DOVER · THRIFT · EDITIONS

The Luck of Roaring Camp and Other Short Stories

BRET HARTE

DOVER PUBLICATIONS, INC.
New York

DOVER THRIFT EDITIONS
EDITOR: STANLEY APPELBAUM

Published in Canada by General Publishing Company, Ltd.,
30 Lesmill Road, Don Mills, Toronto, Ontario.

This Dover edition, first published in 1992,
is a new selection of stories from the volumes
The Luck of Roaring Camp, and Other Sketches
(originally published by Fields, Osgood, & Co., Boston, 1870)
and *A Protégée of Jack Hamlin's; and Other Stories*
(originally published by Houghton, Mifflin and Co., Boston, 1894).
See the table of contents and the
new Note for further details.

Manufactured in the United States of America
Dover Publications, Inc.
31 East 2nd Street
Mineola, N.Y. 11501

Library of Congress Cataloging-in-Publication Data

Harte, Bret, 1836–1902.
The luck of Roaring Camp and other short stories / Bret Harte.
p. cm. — (Dover thrift editions)
Contents: The luck of Roaring Camp — The outcasts of Poker Flat —
Tennessee's partner — M'liss — An ingenue of the Sierras — A
protegee of Jack Hamlin's.
ISBN 0-486-27271-0 (pbk.)
1. Western stories. I. Title. II. Series.
PS1824 1992
813'.4—dc20   92-29395
                                CIP

Note

THE AMERICAN WRITER BRET (FRANCIS BRETT) HARTE (1836–1902) was born in New York State, and lived in California from 1854 to 1871 only; from 1878 to his death he generally resided abroad, chiefly in London. But all his life he continued to write about California and the Far West. Often credited as the inventor of American local-color fiction (though heavily influenced by Dickens), he certainly was the creator of many a durable archetype of the "Western" genre. Even in the present brief anthology we run across the loyal sidekick, the dashing outlaw and his daring woman, the canny stage driver, the tough men softened by contact with women and infants, the undesirable characters being escorted out of town by prudes, the benevolent riverboat gambler and countless hearts of gold beneath rough exteriors. There is an abundance of ironic humor, and many of the stories have a special twist, making Harte an inspiration for O. Henry as well as a predecessor of Owen Wister, Zane Grey and so many others.

The version of "M'liss" reprinted here is the original short version Harte published in the San Francisco weekly *The Golden Era* in two installments in December 1860. Three years later the *Golden Era* editor requested a longer version for serialization; although this new version ran for some three months, Harte later stated that he had finished it off too abruptly. When he first gathered California stories into a volume (the immensely successful *The Luck of Roaring Camp, and Other Sketches*, 1870), he included the original short version of "M'liss" and retained it through several editions. It was only later, in a collected works edition, that he replaced it with the longer version that is still generally reprinted today. (The short version was actually called "Mliss," but in the present edition we have added the well-established apostrophe to avoid the appearance of having made an error.)

The last two stories in this anthology are highly regarded works from Harte's full maturity. It is hoped that the author's way of referring to black people in "A Protégée of Jack Hamlin's" will not offend present-day readers. His affection for, and admiration of, his black characters are obvious from the story, and it is only in fairly recent years that the stereotypes in which he indulges and the vocabulary he uses have fortunately dropped out of circulation.

Contents

From *The Luck of Roaring Camp, and Other Sketches* (1870)

    The Luck of Roaring Camp   1

    The Outcasts of Poker Flat   11

    Tennessee's Partner   21

    M'liss [Mliss; the original short version]   29

From A *Protégée of Jack Hamlin's; and Other Stories* (1894)

    An Ingénue of the Sierras   51

    A Protégée of Jack Hamlin's   67

The Luck of Roaring Camp

THERE WAS COMMOTION in Roaring Camp. It could not have been a fight, for in 1850 that was not novel enough to have called together the entire settlement. The ditches and claims were not only deserted, but "Tuttle's grocery" had contributed its gamblers, who, it will be remembered, calmly continued their game the day that French Pete and Kanaka Joe shot each other to death over the bar in the front room. The whole camp was collected before a rude cabin on the outer edge of the clearing. Conversation was carried on in a low tone, but the name of a woman was frequently repeated. It was a name familiar enough in the camp,— "Cherokee Sal."

Perhaps the less said of her the better. She was a coarse, and, it is to be feared, a very sinful woman. But at that time she was the only woman in Roaring Camp, and was just then lying in sore extremity, when she most needed the ministration of her own sex. Dissolute, abandoned, and irreclaimable, she was yet suffering a martyrdom hard enough to bear even when veiled by sympathizing womanhood, but now terrible in her loneliness. The primal curse had come to her in that original isolation which must have made the punishment of the first transgression so dreadful. It was, perhaps, part of the expiation of her sin, that, at a moment when she most lacked her sex's intuitive tenderness and care, she met only the half-contemptuous faces of her masculine associates. Yet a few of the spectators were, I think, touched by her sufferings. Sandy Tipton thought it was "rough on Sal," and, in the contemplation of her condition, for a moment rose superior to the fact that he had an ace and two bowers in his sleeve.

It will be seen, also, that the situation was novel. Deaths were by no means uncommon in Roaring Camp, but a birth was a new thing. People had been dismissed from the camp effectively, finally, and with no possibility of return; but this was the first time that anybody had been introduced *ab initio*. Hence the excitement.

1

"You go in there, Stumpy," said a prominent citizen known as "Kentuck," addressing one of the loungers. "Go in there, and see what you kin do. You've had experience in them things."

Perhaps there was a fitness in the selection. Stumpy, in other climes, had been the putative head of two families; in fact, it was owing to some legal informality in these proceedings that Roaring Camp—a city of refuge—was indebted to his company. The crowd approved the choice, and Stumpy was wise enough to bow to the majority. The door closed on the extempore surgeon and midwife, and Roaring Camp sat down outside, smoked its pipe, and awaited the issue.

The assemblage numbered about a hundred men. One or two of these were actual fugitives from justice, some were criminal, and all were reckless. Physically, they exhibited no indication of their past lives and character. The greatest scamp had a Raphael face, with a profusion of blond hair; Oakhurst, a gambler, had the melancholy air and intellectual abstraction of a Hamlet; the coolest and most courageous man was scarcely over five feet in height, with a soft voice and an embarrassed, timid manner. The term "roughs" applied to them was a distinction rather than a definition. Perhaps in the minor details of fingers, toes, ears, &c., the camp may have been deficient; but these slight omissions did not detract from their aggregate force. The strongest man had but three fingers on his right hand; the best shot had but one eye.

Such was the physical aspect of the men that were dispersed around the cabin. The camp lay in a triangular valley, between two hills and a river. The only outlet was a steep trail over the summit of a hill that faced the cabin, now illuminated by the rising moon. The suffering woman might have seen it from the rude bunk whereon she lay,—seen it winding like a silver thread until it was lost in the stars above.

A fire of withered pine-boughs added sociability to the gathering. By degrees the natural levity of Roaring Camp returned. Bets were freely offered and taken regarding the result. Three to five that "Sal would get through with it;" even that the child would survive; side bets as to the sex and complexion of the coming stranger. In the midst of an excited discussion an exclamation came from those nearest the door, and the camp stopped to listen. Above the swaying and moaning of the pines, the swift rush of the river, and the crackling of the fire, rose a sharp, querulous cry—a cry unlike anything heard before in the camp. The pines stopped moaning, the river ceased to rush, and the fire to crackle. It seemed as if Nature had stopped to listen too.

The camp rose to its feet as one man! It was proposed to explode a barrel of gunpowder, but, in consideration of the situation of the mother, better counsels prevailed, and only a few revolvers were discharged; for, whether owing to the rude surgery of the camp, or some other reason, Cherokee Sal was sinking fast. Within an hour she had climbed, as it were, that rugged road that led to the stars, and so passed out of Roaring Camp, its sin and shame, for ever. I do not think that the announcement disturbed them much, except in speculation as to the fate of the child. "Can he live now?" was asked of Stumpy. The answer was doubtful. The only other being of Cherokee Sal's sex and maternal condition in the settlement was an ass. There was some conjecture as to fitness, but the experiment was tried. It was less problematical than the ancient treatment of Romulus and Remus, and apparently as successful.

When these details were completed, which exhausted another hour, the door was opened, and the anxious crowd of men who had already formed themselves into a queue, entered in single file. Beside the low bunk or shelf, on which the figure of the mother was starkly outlined below the blankets, stood a pine table. On this a candle-box was placed, and within it, swathed in staring red flannel, lay the last arrival at Roaring Camp. Beside the candle-box was placed a hat. Its use was soon indicated. "Gentlemen," said Stumpy, with a singular mixture of authority and *ex officio* complacency,—"Gentlemen will please pass in at the front door, round the table, and out at the back door. Them as wishes to contribute anything toward the orphan will find a hat handy." The first man entered with his hat on; he uncovered, however, as he looked about him, and so, unconsciously, set an example to the next. In such communities good and bad actions are catching. As the procession filed in, comments were audible,—criticisms addressed, perhaps, rather to Stumpy, in the character of showman,—"Is that him?" "mighty small specimen;" "hasn't mor'n got the color;" "ain't bigger nor a derringer." The contributions were as characteristic: A silver tobacco-box; a doubloon; a navy revolver, silver mounted; a gold specimen; a very beautifully embroidered lady's handkerchief from Oakhurst (the gambler); a diamond breastpin; a diamond ring (suggested by the pin, with the remark from the giver that he "saw that pin and went two diamonds better"); a slung shot; a Bible (contributor not detected); a golden spur; a silver teaspoon (the initials, I regret to say, were not the giver's); a pair of surgeon's shears; a lancet; a Bank of England note for £5; and about $200 in loose gold and silver coin. During these proceedings Stumpy maintained a silence as impassive as the dead on his left, a gravity as inscrutable as that of the newly born on his right. Only one incident occurred to break the monotony of the curious procession. As Kentuck bent over the candle-box half curiously, the child turned, and, in a spasm of pain, caught at his groping finger, and held it fast for a moment. Kentuck looked foolish and embarrassed. Something like a blush tried to assert itself in his weather-beaten cheek. "The d—d little cuss!" he said, as he extricated his finger, with, perhaps, more tenderness and care than he might have been deemed capable of showing. He held that finger a little apart from its fellows as he went out, and examined it curiously. The examination provoked the same original remark in regard to the child. In fact, he seemed to enjoy repeating it. "He rastled with my finger," he remarked to Tipton, holding up the member, "the d—d little cuss!"

It was four o'clock before the camp sought repose. A light burnt in the cabin where the watchers sat, for Stumpy did not go to bed that night. Nor did Kentuck. He drank quite freely, and related with great gusto his experience, invariably ending with his characteristic condemnation of the new-comer. It seemed to relieve him of any unjust implication of sentiment, and Kentuck had the weaknesses of the nobler sex. When everybody else had gone to bed, he walked down to the river, and whistled reflectingly. Then he walked up the gulch, past the cabin, still whistling with demonstrative unconcern. At a large red-wood tree he paused and retraced his steps, and again passed the cabin. Half-way down to the river's bank he again paused, and then returned and knocked at the door. It was opened by Stumpy. "How goes it?" said Kentuck, looking past Stumpy toward the candle-box. "All serene," replied Stumpy. "Anything up?" "Nothing." There was a pause—an embarrassing one— Stumpy still holding the door. Then Kentuck had recourse to his finger, which he held up to Stumpy. "Rastled with it,—the d—d little cuss," he said, and retired.

The next day Cherokee Sal had such rude sepulture as Roaring Camp afforded. After her body had been committed to the hill-side, there was a formal meeting of the camp to discuss what should be done with her infant. A resolution to adopt it was unanimous and enthusiastic. But an animated discussion in regard to the manner and feasibility of providing for its wants at once sprung up. It was remarkable that the argument partook of none of those fierce personalities with which discussions were usually conducted at Roaring Camp. Tipton proposed that they should send the child to Red Dog,—a distance of forty miles,—where female attention could be procured. But the unlucky suggestion met with fierce and unanimous opposition. It was evident that no plan which entailed parting from their new acquisition would for a moment be entertained. "Besides," said Tom Ryder, "them fellows at Red Dog would swap it, and ring in somebody else on us." A disbelief in the honesty of other camps prevailed at Roaring Camp as in other places.

The introduction of a female nurse in the camp also met with objection. It was argued that no decent woman could be prevailed to accept Roaring Camp as her home, and the speaker urged that "they didn't want any more of the other kind." This unkind allusion to the defunct mother, harsh as it may seem, was the first spasm of propriety,—the first symptom of the camp's regeneration. Stumpy advanced nothing. Perhaps he felt a certain delicacy in interfering with the selection of a possible successor in office. But when questioned, he averred stoutly that he and "Jinny"—the mammal before alluded to—could manage to rear the child. There was something original, independent, and heroic about the plan that pleased the camp. Stumpy was retained. Certain articles were sent for to Sacramento. "Mind," said the treasurer, as he pressed a bag of gold-dust into the expressman's hand, "the best that can be got,—lace, you know, and filigree-work and frills—d—n the cost!"

Strange to say, the child thrived. Perhaps the invigorating climate of the mountain camp was compensation for material deficiencies. Nature took the foundling to her broader breast. In that rare atmosphere of the Sierra foothills,—that air pungént with balsamic odour, that ethereal cordial at once bracing and exhilarating,—he may have found food and nourishment, or a subtle chemistry that transmuted asses' milk to lime and phosphorus. Stumpy inclined to the belief that it was the latter, and good nursing. "Me and that ass," he would say, "has been father and mother to him! Don't you," he would add, apostrophizing the helpless bundle before him, "never go back on us."

By the time he was a month old, the necessity of giving him a name became apparent. He had generally been known as "the Kid," "Stumpy's boy," "the Cayote" (an allusion to his vocal powers), and even by Kentuck's endearing diminutive of "the d—d little cuss." But these were felt to be vague and unsatisfactory, and were at last dismissed under another influence. Gamblers and adventurers are generally superstitious, and Oakhurst one day declared that the baby had brought "the luck" to Roaring Camp. It was certain that of late they had been successful. "Luck" was the name agreed upon, with the prefix of Tommy for greater convenience. No allusion was made to the mother, and the father was unknown. "It's better," said the philosophical Oakhurst, "to take a fresh deal all round. Call him Luck, and start him fair." A day was accordingly set apart for the christening. What was meant by this ceremony the reader may imagine, who has already gathered some idea of the reckless irreverence of Roaring Camp. The master of ceremonies was one "Boston," a noted wag, and the occasion seemed to promise the greatest facetiousness. This ingenious satirist had spent two days in preparing a burlesque of the church service, with pointed local allusions. The choir was properly trained, and Sandy Tipton was to stand godfather. But after the procession had marched to the grove with music and banners, and the child had been deposited before a mock altar, Stumpy stepped before the expectant crowd. "It ain't my style to spoil fun, boys," said the little man, stoutly, eyeing the faces around him, "but it strikes me that this thing ain't exactly on the squar. It's playing it pretty low down on this yer baby to ring in fun on him that he ain't going to understand. And ef there's going to be any godfathers round, I'd like to see who's got any better rights than me." A silence followed Stumpy's speech. To the credit of all humorists be it said, that the first man to acknowledge its justice was the satirist, thus stopped of his fun. "But," said Stumpy, quickly, following up his advantage, "we're here for a christening, and we'll have it. I proclaim you Thomas Luck, according to the laws of the United States and the State of California, so help me God." It was the first time that the name of the Deity had been uttered otherwise than profanely in the camp. The form of christening was perhaps even more ludicrous than the satirist had conceived; but, strangely enough, nobody saw it, and nobody laughed. "Tommy" was christened as seriously as he would have been under a Christian roof, and cried and was comforted in as orthodox fashion.

And so the work of regeneration began in Roaring Camp. Almost imperceptibly a change came over the settlement. The cabin assigned to "Tommy Luck"—or "The Luck," as he was more frequently called—first showed signs of improvement. It was kept scrupulously clean and white-washed. Then it was boarded, clothed, and papered. The rosewood cradle—packed eighty miles by mule—had, in Stumpy's way of putting it, "sorter killed the rest of the furniture." So the rehabilitation of the cabin became a necessity. The men who were in the habit of lounging in at Stumpy's to see "how 'The Luck' got on" seemed to appreciate the change, and, in self-defense, the rival establishment of "Tuttle's grocery" bestirred itself, and imported a carpet and mirrors. The reflections of the latter on the appearance of Roaring Camp tended to produce stricter habits of personal cleanliness. Again, Stumpy imposed a kind of quarantine upon those who aspired to the honor and privilege of holding "The Luck." It was a cruel mortification to Kentuck—who, in the carelessness of a large nature and the habits of frontier life, had begun to regard all garments as a second cuticle, which, like a snake's, only sloughed off through decay—to be debarred this privilege from certain prudential reasons. Yet such was the subtle influence of innovation that he thereafter appeared regularly every afternoon in a clean shirt, and face still shining from his ablutions. Nor were moral and social sanitary laws neglected. "Tommy," who was supposed to spend his whole existence in a persistent attempt to repose, must not be disturbed by noise. The shouting and yelling which had gained the camp its infelicitous title were not permitted within hearing distance of Stumpy's. The men conversed in whispers, or smoked with Indian gravity. Profanity was tacitly given up in these sacred precincts, and throughout the camp a popular form of expletive, known as "D——n the luck!" and "Curse the luck!" was abandoned, as having a new personal bearing. Vocal music was not interdicted, being supposed to have a soothing, tranquillizing quality, and one song, sung by "Man-o'-war Jack," an English sailor, from her Majesty's Australian colonies, was quite popular as a lullaby. It was a lugubrious recital of the exploits of "the Arethusa, Seventy-four," in a muffled minor, ending with a prolonged dying fall at the burden of each verse, "On b-o-o-o-ard of the Arethusa." It was a fine sight to see Jack holding The Luck, rocking from side to side as if with the motion of a ship, and crooning forth this naval ditty. Either through the peculiar rocking of Jack or the length of his song—it contained ninety stanzas, and was continued with conscientious deliberation to the bitter end—the lullaby generally had the desired effect. At such times the men would lie at full length under the trees, in the soft summer twilight, smoking their pipes and drinking in the melodious utterances. An indistinct idea that this was pastoral happiness pervaded the camp. "This 'ere kind o' think," said the Cockney Simmons, meditatively reclining on his elbow, "is 'evingly." It reminded him of Greenwich.

On the long summer days The Luck was usually carried to the gulch, from whence the golden store of Roaring Camp was taken. There, on a blanket spread over pine-boughs, he would lie while the men were working in the ditches below. Latterly there was a rude attempt to decorate this bower with flowers and sweet-smelling shrubs, and generally someone would bring him a cluster of wild honeysuckles, azaleas, or the painted blossoms of Las Mariposas. The men had suddenly awakened to the fact that there were beauty and significance in these trifles, which they had so long trodden carelessly beneath their feet. A flake of glittering mica, a fragment of variegated quartz, a bright pebble from the bed of the creek, became beautiful to eyes thus cleared and strengthened, and were invariably put aside for "The Luck." It was wonderful how many treasures the woods and hill-sides yielded that "would do for Tommy." Surrounded by playthings such as never child out of fairy-land had before, it is to be hoped that Tommy was content. He appeared to be securely happy, albeit there was an infantine gravity about him, a contemplative light in his round gray eyes, that sometimes worried Stumpy. He was always tractable and quiet, and it is recorded that once, having crept beyond his "corral,"—a hedge of tessellated pine-boughs, which surrounded his bed,—he dropped over the bank on his head in the soft earth, and remained with his mottled legs in the air in that position for at least five minutes with unflinching gravity. He was extricated without a murmur. I hesitate to record the many other instances of his sagacity, which rest, unfortunately, upon the statements of prejudiced friends. Some of them were not without a tinge of superstition. "I crep' up the bank just now," said Kentuck, one day, in a breathless state of excitement, "and dern my skin if he wasn't a talking to a jay-bird as was a sittin' on his lap. There they was, just as free and sociable as anything you please, a jawin' at each other just like two cherry-bums." Howbeit, whether creeping over the pine-boughs or lying lazily on his back blinking at the leaves above him, to him the birds sang, the squirrels chattered, and the flowers bloomed. Nature was his nurse and playfellow. For him she would let slip between the leaves golden shafts of sunlight that fell just within his grasp; she would send wandering breezes to visit him with the balm of bay and resinous gums; to him the tall red-woods nodded familiarly and sleepily, the bumble-bees buzzed, and the rooks cawed a slumberous accompaniment.

Such was the golden summer of Roaring Camp. They were "flush times,"—and the luck was with them. The claims had yielded enormously. The camp was jealous of its privileges, and looked suspiciously on strangers. No encouragement was given to immigration, and, to make their seclusion more perfect, the land on either side of the mountain-wall that surrounded the camp they duly pre-empted. This, and a reputation for singular proficiency with the revolver, kept the reserve of Roaring Camp inviolate. The expressman—their only connecting link with the surrounding world—sometimes told wonderful stories of the camp. He would say, "They've a street up there in 'Roaring,' that would lay over any street in Red Dog. They've got vines and flowers round their houses, and they wash themselves twice a day. But they're mighty rough on strangers, and they worship an Ingin baby."

With the prosperity of the camp came a desire for further improvement. It was proposed to build a hotel in the following spring, and to invite one or two decent families to reside there for the sake of "The Luck,"—who might perhaps profit by female companionship. The sacrifice that this concession to the sex cost these men, who were fiercely sceptical in regard to its general virtue and usefulness, can only be accounted for by their affection for Tommy. A few still held out. But the resolve could not be carried into effect for three months, and the minority meekly yielded in the hope that something might turn up to prevent it. And it did.

The winter of 1851 will long be remembered in the foot-hills. The snow lay deep on the Sierras, and every mountain creek became a river, and every river a lake. Each gorge and gulch was transformed into a tumultuous water-course that descended the hill-sides, tearing down giant trees, and scattering its drift and débris along the plain. Red Dog had been twice under water, and Roaring Camp had been forewarned. "Water put the gold into them gulches," said Stumpy; "it's been here once and will be here again!" And that night the North Fork suddenly leaped over its banks, and swept up the triangular valley of Roaring Camp.

In the confusion of rushing water, crushing trees, and crackling timber, and the darkness which seemed to flow with the water and blot out the fair valley, but little could be done to collect the scattered camp. When the morning broke, the cabin of Stumpy nearest the river-bank was gone. Higher up the gulch they found the body of its unlucky owner; but the pride, the hope, the joy, the Luck of Roaring Camp had disappeared. They were returning with sad hearts, when a shout from the bank recalled them.

It was a relief-boat from down the river. They had picked up, they said, a man and an infant, nearly exhausted, about two miles below. Did anybody know them, and did they belong here?

It needed but a glance to show them Kentuck lying there, cruelly crushed and bruised, but still holding the Luck of Roaring Camp in his arms. As they bent over the strangely assorted pair, they saw that the child was cold and pulseless. "He is dead," said one. Kentuck opened his eyes. "Dead?" he repeated, feebly. "Yes, my man, and you are dying too." A smile lit the eyes of the expiring Kentuck. "Dying," he repeated, "he's a taking me with him,—tell the boys I've got the Luck with me now;" and the strong man, clinging to the frail babe as a drowning man is said to cling to a straw, drifted away into the shadowy river that flows for ever to the unknown sea.

The Outcasts of Poker Flat

As Mr. John Oakhurst, gambler, stepped into the main street of Poker Flat on the morning of the twenty-third of November, 1850, he was conscious of a change in its moral atmosphere since the preceding night. Two or three men, conversing earnestly together, ceased as he approached, and exchanged significant glances. There was a Sabbath lull in the air, which, in a settlement unused to Sabbath influences, looked ominous.

Mr. Oakhurst's calm, handsome face betrayed small concern in these indications. Whether he was conscious of any predisposing cause, was another question. "I reckon they're after somebody," he reflected; "likely it's me." He returned to his pocket the handkerchief with which he had been whipping away the red dust of Poker Flat from his neat boots, and quietly discharged his mind of any further conjecture.

In point of fact, Poker Flat was "after somebody." It had lately suffered the loss of several thousand dollars, two valuable horses, and a prominent citizen. It was experiencing a spasm of virtuous reaction, quite as lawless and ungovernable as any of the acts that had provoked it. A secret committee had determined to rid the town of all improper persons. This was done permanently in regard of two men who were then hanging from the boughs of a sycamore in the gulch, and temporarily in the banishment of certain other objectionable characters. I regret to say that some of these were ladies. It is but due to the sex, however, to state that their impropriety was professional, and it was only in such easily established standards of evil that Poker Flat ventured to sit in judgment.

Mr. Oakhurst was right in supposing that he was included in this category. A few of the committee had urged hanging him as a possible example, and a sure method of reimbursing themselves from his pockets of the sums he had won from them. "It's agin justice," said Jim Wheeler, "to let this yer young man from Roaring Camp—an entire stranger—

carry away our money." But a crude sentiment of equity residing in the breasts of those who had been fortunate enough to win from Mr. Oakhurst overruled this narrower local prejudice.

Mr. Oakhurst received his sentence with philosophic calmness, none the less coolly that he was aware of the hesitation of his judges. He was too much of a gambler not to accept Fate. With him life was at best an uncertain game, and he recognized the usual per-centage in favor of the dealer.

A party of armed men accompanied the deported wickedness of Poker Flat to the outskirts of the settlement. Besides Mr. Oakhurst, who was known to be a coolly desperate man, and for whose intimidation the armed escort was intended, the expatriated party consisted of a young woman familiarly known as "The Duchess;" another, who had bore the title of "Mother Shipton;" and "Uncle Billy," a suspected sluice-robber and confirmed drunkard. The cavalcade provoked no comments from the spectators, nor was any word uttered by the escort. Only when the gulch which marked the uttermost limit of Poker Flat was reached, the leader spoke briefly and to the point. The exiles were forbidden to return at the peril of their lives.

As the escort disappeared, their pent-up feelings found vent in a few hysterical tears from the Duchess, some bad language from Mother Shipton, and a Parthian volley of expletives from Uncle Billy. The philosophic Oakhurst alone remained silent. He listened calmly to Mother Shipton's desire to cut somebody's heart out, to the repeated statements of the Duchess that she would die in the road, and to the alarming oaths that seemed to be bumped out of Uncle Billy as he rode forward. With the easy good-humor characteristic of his class, he insisted upon exchanging his own riding-horse, "Five Spot," for the sorry mule which the Duchess rode. But even this act did not draw the party into any closer sympathy. The young woman readjusted her somewhat draggled plumes with a feeble, faded coquetry; Mother Shipton eyed the possessor of "Five Spot" with malevolence; and Uncle Billy included the whole party in one sweeping anathema.

The road to Sandy Bar—a camp that, not having as yet experienced the regenerating influences of Poker Flat, consequently seemed to offer some invitation to the emigrants—lay over a steep mountain range. It was distant a day's severe travel. In that advanced season, the party soon passed out of the moist, temperate regions of the foot-hills into the dry, cold, bracing air of the Sierras. The trail was narrow and difficult. At noon the Duchess, rolling out of her saddle upon the ground, declared her intention of going no farther, and the party halted.

The spot was singularly wild and impressive. A wooded amphitheatre, surrounded on three sides by precipitous cliffs of naked granite, sloped gently towards the crest of another precipice that overlooked the valley. It was, undoubtedly, the most suitable spot for a camp, had camping been advisable. But Mr. Oakhurst knew that scarcely half the journey to Sandy Bar was accomplished, and the party were not equipped or provisioned for delay. This fact he pointed out to his companions curtly, with a philosophic commentary on the folly of "throwing up their hand before the game was played out." But they were furnished with liquor, which in this emergency stood them in place of food, fuel, rest, and prescience. In spite of his remonstrances, it was not long before they were more or less under its influence. Uncle Billy passed rapidly from a bellicose state into one of stupor, the Duchess became maudlin, and Mother Shipton snored. Mr. Oakhurst alone remained erect, leaning against a rock, calmly surveying them.

Mr. Oakhurst did not drink. It interfered with a profession which required coolness, impassiveness, and presence of mind, and, in his own language, he "couldn't afford it." As he gazed at his recumbent fellow-exiles, the loneliness begotten of his pariah-trade, his habits of life, his very vices, for the first time seriously oppressed him. He bestirred himself in dusting his black clothes, washing his hands and face, and other acts characteristic of his studiously neat habits, and for a moment forgot his annoyance. The thought of deserting his weaker and more pitiable companions never perhaps occurred to him. Yet he could not help feeling the want of that excitement which, singularly enough, was most conducive to that calm equanimity for which he was notorious. He looked at the gloomy walls that rose a thousand feet sheer above the circling pines around him; at the sky, ominously clouded; at the valley below, already deepening into shadow. And, doing so, suddenly he heard his own name called.

A horseman slowly ascended the trail. In the fresh, open face of the new-comer, Mr. Oakhurst recognized Tom Simson, otherwise known as "The Innocent" of Sandy Bar. He had met him some months before over a "little game," and had, with perfect equanimity, won the entire fortune—amounting to some forty dollars—of that guileless youth. After the game was finished, Mr. Oakhurst drew the youthful speculator behind the door, and thus addressed him: "Tommy, you're a good little man, but you can't gamble worth a cent. Don't try it over again." He then handed him his money back, pushed him gently from the room, and so made a devoted slave of Tom Simson.

There was a remembrance of this in his boyish and enthusiastic greeting of Mr. Oakhurst. He had started, he said, to go to Poker Flat to seek his fortune. "Alone?" No, not exactly alone; in fact (a giggle), he had run away with Piney Woods. Didn't Mr. Oakhurst remember Piney? She that used to wait on the table at the Temperance House? They had been engaged a long time, but old Jake Woods had objected, and so they had run away, and were going to Poker Flat to be married; and here they were. And they were tired out, and how lucky it was they had found a place to camp and company. All this the Innocent delivered rapidly, while Piney, a stout, comely damsel of fifteen, emerged from behind the pine-tree, where she had been blushing unseen, and rode to the side of her lover.

Mr. Oakhurst seldom troubled himself with sentiment, still less with propriety; but he had a vague idea that the situation was not fortunate. He retained, however, his presence of mind sufficiently to kick Uncle Billy, who was about to say something, and Uncle Billy was sober enough to recognize in Mr. Oakhurst's kick a superior power that would not bear trifling. He then endeavored to dissuade Tom Simson from delaying further, but in vain. He even pointed out the fact that there was no provision, nor means of making a camp. But, unluckily, the Innocent met this objection by assuring the party that he was provided with an extra mule loaded with provisions, and by the discovery of a rude attempt at a log-house near the trail. "Piney can stay with Mrs. Oakhurst," said the Innocent, pointing to the Duchess, "and I can shift for myself."

Nothing but Mr. Oakhurst's admonishing foot saved Uncle Billy from bursting into a roar of laughter. As it was, he felt compelled to retire up the cañon until he could recover his gravity. There he confided the joke to the tall pine-trees, with many slaps of his leg, contortions of his face, and the usual profanity. But when he returned to the party, he found them seated by a fire—for the air had grown strangely chill, and the sky overcast—in apparently amicable conversation. Piney was actually talking in an impulsive, girlish fashion to the Duchess, who was listening with an interest and animation she had not shown for many days. The Innocent was holding forth, apparently with equal effect, to Mr. Oakhurst and Mother Shipton, who was actually relaxing into amiability. "Is this yer a d—d pic-nic?" said Uncle Billy, with inward scorn, as he surveyed the sylvan group, the glancing firelight, and the tethered animals in the foreground. Suddenly an idea mingled with the alcoholic fumes that disturbed his brain. It was apparently of a jocular nature, for he felt impelled to slap his leg again and cram his fist into his mouth.

As the shadows crept slowly up the mountain, a slight breeze rocked the tops of the pine-trees, and moaned through their long and gloomy aisles. The ruined cabin, patched and covered with pine-boughs, was set apart for the ladies. As the lovers parted, they unaffectedly exchanged a kiss, so honest and sincere that it might have been heard above the swaying pines. The frail Duchess and the malevolent Mother Shipton were probably too stunned to remark upon this last evidence of simplicity, and so turned without a word to the hut. The fire was replenished, the men lay down before the door, and in a few minutes were asleep.

Mr. Oakhurst was a light sleeper. Toward morning he awoke benumbed and cold. As he stirred the dying fire, the wind, which was now blowing strongly, brought to his cheek that which caused the blood to leave it—snow!

He started to his feet with the intention of awakening the sleepers, for there was no time to lose. But turning to where Uncle Billy had been lying, he found him gone. A suspicion leaped to his brain and a curse to his lips. He ran to the spot where the mules had been tethered; they were no longer there. The tracks were already rapidly disappearing in the snow.

The momentary excitement brought Mr. Oakhurst back to the fire with his usual calm. He did not waken the sleepers. The Innocent slumbered peacefully, with a smile on his good-humored, freckled face; the virgin Piney slept beside her frailer sisters as sweetly as though attended by celestial guardians, and Mr. Oakhurst, drawing his blanket over his shoulders, stroked his mustaches and waited for the dawn. It came slowly in a whirling mist of snow-flakes, that dazzled and confused the eye. What could be seen of the landscape appeared magically changed. He looked over the valley, and summed up the present and future in two words—"snowed in!"

A careful inventory of the provisions, which, fortunately for the party, had been stored within the hut, and so escaped the felonious fingers of Uncle Billy, disclosed the fact that with care and prudence they might last ten days longer. "That is," said Mr. Oakhurst, *sotto voce* to the Innocent, "if you're willing to board us. If you ain't—and perhaps you'd better not—you can wait till Uncle Billy gets back with provisions." For some occult reason Mr. Oakhurst could not bring himself to disclose Uncle Billy's rascality, and so offered the hypothesis that he had wandered from the camp and had accidentally stampeded the animals. He dropped a warning to the Duchess and Mother Shipton, who of course knew the facts of their associate's defection. "They'll find out the truth about us *all* when they find out anything," he added significantly, "and there's no good frightening them now."

Tom Simson not only put all his worldly store at the disposal of Mr. Oakhurst, but seemed to enjoy the prospect of their enforced seclusion. "We'll have a good camp for a week, and then the snow'll melt, and we'll all go back together." The cheerful gaiety of the young man, and Mr. Oakhurst's calm, infected the others. The Innocent, with the aid of pine-boughs, extemporized a thatch for the roofless cabin, and the Duchess directed Piney in the rearrangement of the interior with a taste and tact that opened the blue eyes of that provincial maiden to their fullest extent. "I reckon now you're used to fine things at Poker Flat," said Piney. The Duchess turned away sharply to conceal something that reddened her cheeks through its professional tint, and Mother Shipton requested Piney not to "chatter." But when Mr. Oakhurst returned from a weary search for the trail, he heard the sound of happy laughter echoed from the rocks. He stopped in some alarm, and his thoughts first naturally reverted to the whiskey, which he had prudently cached. "And yet it don't somehow sound like whiskey," said the gambler. It was not until he caught sight of the blazing fire through the still blinding storm and the group around it, that he settled to the conviction that it was "square fun."

Whether Mr. Oakhurst had cached his cards with the whiskey as something debarred the free access of the community, I cannot say. It was certain that, in Mother Shipton's words, he "didn't say cards once" during that evening. Haply the time was beguiled by an accordion, produced somewhat ostentatiously by Tom Simson from his pack. Notwithstanding some difficulties attending the manipulation of this instrument, Piney Woods managed to pluck several reluctant melodies from its keys, to an accompaniment by the Innocent on a pair of bone castanets. But the crowning festivity of the evening was reached in a rude campmeeting hymn, which the lovers, joining hands, sang with great earnestness and vociferation. I fear that a certain defiant tone and Covenanter's swing to its chorus, rather than any devotional quality, caused it speedily to infect the others, who at last joined in the refrain:—

> "I'm proud to live in the service of the Lord,
> And I'm bound to die in His army."

The pines rocked, the storm eddied and whirled above the miserable group, and the flames of their altar leaped heavenward, as if in token of the vow.

At midnight the storm abated, the rolling clouds parted, and the stars glittered keenly above the sleeping camp. Mr. Oakhurst, whose professional habits had enabled him to live on the smallest possible amount of sleep, in dividing the watch with Tom Simson, somehow managed to take upon himself the greater part of that duty. He excused himself to the Innocent by saying that he had "often been a week without sleep." "Doing what?" asked Tom. "Poker!" replied Oakhurst, sententiously; "when a man gets a streak of luck—nigger-luck—he don't get tired. The luck gives in first. Luck," continued the gambler, reflectively, "is a mighty queer thing. All you know about it for certain is that it's bound to change. And it's finding out when it's going to change that makes you.

We've had a streak of bad luck since we left Poker Flat—you come along, and slap you get into it, too. If you can hold your cards right along you're all right. For," added the gambler, with cheerful irrelevance—

> " 'I'm proud to live in the service of the Lord,
> And I'm bound to die in His army.' "

The third day came, and the sun, looking through the white-curtained valley, saw the outcasts divide their slowly decreasing store of provisions for the morning meal. It was one of the peculiarities of that mountain climate that its rays diffused a kindly warmth over the wintry landscape, as if in regretful commiseration of the past. But it revealed drift on drift of snow piled high around the hut—a hopeless, uncharted, trackless sea of white lying below the rocky shores to which the castaways still clung. Through the marvellously clear air the smoke of the pastoral village of Poker Flat rose miles away. Mother Shipton saw it, and from a remote pinnacle of her rocky fastness, hurled in that direction a final malediction. It was her last vituperative attempt, and perhaps for that reason was invested with a certain degree of sublimity. It did her good, she privately informed the Duchess. "Just you go out there and cuss, and see." She then set herself to the task of amusing "the child," as she and the Duchess were pleased to call Piney. Piney was no chicken, but it was a soothing and original theory of the pair thus to account for the fact that she didn't swear and wasn't improper.

When night crept up again through the gorges, the reedy notes of the accordion rose and fell in fitful spasms and long-drawn gasps by the flickering camp-fire. But music failed to fill entirely the aching void left by insufficient food, and a new diversion was proposed by Piney—storytelling. Neither Mr. Oakhurst nor his female companions caring to relate their personal experiences, this plan would have failed, too, but for the Innocent. Some months before he had chanced upon a stray copy of Mr. Pope's ingenious translation of the Iliad. He now proposed to narrate the principal incidents of that poem—having thoroughly mastered the argument and fairly forgotten the words—in the current vernacular of Sandy Bar. And so for the rest of that night the Homeric demigods again walked the earth. Trojan bully and wily Greek wrestled in the winds, and the great pines in the cañon seemed to bow to the wrath of the son of Peleus. Mr. Oakhurst listened with quiet satisfaction. Most especially was he interested in the fate of "Ash-heels," as the Innocent persisted in denominating the "swift-footed Achilles."

So with small food and much of Homer and the accordion, a week passed over the heads of the outcasts. The sun again forsook them, and again from leaden skies the snow-flakes were sifted over the land. Day by day closer around them drew the snowy circle, until at last they looked from their prison over drifted walls of drizzling white, that towered twenty feet above their heads. It became more and more difficult to replenish their fires, even from the fallen trees beside them, now half hidden in the drifts. And yet no one complained. The lovers turned from the dreary prospect, and looked into each other's eyes, and were happy. Mr. Oakhurst settled himself coolly to the losing game before him. The Duchess, more cheerful than she had been, assumed the care of Piney. Only Mother Shipton—once the strongest of the party—seemed to sicken and fade. At midnight on the tenth day she called Oakhurst to her side. "I'm going," she said, in a voice of querulous weakness, "but don't say anything about it. Don't waken the kids. Take the bundle from under my head and open it." Mr. Oakhurst did so. It contained Mother Shipton's rations for the last week, untouched. "Give 'em to the child," she said, pointing to the sleeping Piney. "You've starved yourself," said the gambler. "That's what they call it," said the woman, querulously, as she lay down again, and, turning her face to the wall, passed quietly away.

The accordion and the bones were put aside that day, and Homer was forgotten. When the body of Mother Shipton had been committed to the snow, Mr. Oakhurst took the Innocent aside, and showed him a pair of snow-shoes, which he had fashioned from the old pack-saddle. "There's one chance in a hundred to save her yet," he said, pointing to Piney; "but it's there," he added, pointing toward Poker Flat. "If you can reach there in two days she's safe." "And you?" asked Tom Simson. "I'll stay here," was the curt reply.

The lovers parted with a long embrace. "You are not going, too?" said the Duchess, as she saw Mr. Oakhurst apparently waiting to accompany him. "As far as the cañon," he replied. He turned suddenly, and kissed the Duchess, leaving her pallid face aflame, and her trembling limbs rigid with amazement.

Night came, but not Mr. Oakhurst. It brought the storm again and the whirling snow. Then the Duchess, feeding the fire, found that some one had quietly piled beside the hut enough fuel to last a few days longer. The tears rose to her eyes, but she hid them from Piney.

The women slept but little. In the morning, looking into each other's faces, they read their fate. Neither spoke; but Piney, accepting the position of the stronger, drew near and placed her arm around the Duchess's waist. They kept this attitude for the rest of the day. That night the storm reached its greatest fury, and, rending asunder the protecting pines, invaded the very hut.

Toward morning they found themselves unable to feed the fire, which gradually died away. As the embers slowly blackened, the Duchess crept closer to Piney, and broke the silence of many hours: "Piney, can you pray?" "No, dear," said Piney, simply. The Duchess, without knowing exactly why, felt relieved, and, putting her head upon Piney's shoulder, spoke no more. And so reclining, the younger and purer pillowing the head of her soiled sister upon her virgin breast, they fell asleep.

The wind lulled as if it feared to waken them. Feathery drifts of snow, shaken from the long pine-boughs, flew like white-winged birds, and settled about them as they slept. The moon through the rifted clouds looked down upon what had been the camp. But all human stain, all trace of earthly travail, was hidden beneath the spotless mantle mercifully flung from above.

They slept all that day and the next, nor did they waken when voices and footsteps broke the silence of the camp. And when pitying fingers brushed the snow from their wan faces, you could scarcely have told, from the equal peace that dwelt upon them, which was she that had sinned. Even the law of Poker Flat recognized this, and turned away, leaving them still locked in each other's arms.

But at the head of the gulch, on one of the largest pine-trees, they found the deuce of clubs pinned to the bark with a bowie-knife. It bore the following, written in pencil, in a firm hand:—

†

BENEATH THIS TREE
LIES THE BODY
OF
JOHN OAKHURST,
WHO STRUCK A STREAK OF BAD LUCK
ON THE 23RD OF NOVEMBER, 1850,
AND
HANDED IN HIS CHECKS
ON THE 7TH DECEMBER, 1850.

†

And pulseless and cold, with a Derringer by his side and a bullet in his heart, though still calm as in life, beneath the snow lay he who was at once the strongest and yet the weakest of the outcasts of Poker Flat.

Tennessee's Partner

I DO NOT think that we ever knew his real name. Our ignorance of it certainly never gave us any social inconvenience, for at Sandy Bar in 1854 most men were christened anew. Sometimes these appellatives were derived from some distinctiveness of dress, as in the case of "Dungaree Jack;" or from some peculiarity of habit, as shown in "Saleratus Bill," so called from an undue proportion of that chemical in his daily bread; or from some unlucky slip, as exhibited in "The Iron Pirate," a mild, inoffensive man, who earned that baleful title by his unfortunate mispronunciation of the term "iron pyrites." Perhaps this may have been the beginning of a rude heraldry; but I am constrained to think that it was because a man's real name in that day rested solely upon his own unsupported statement. "Call yourself Clifford, do you?" said Boston, addressing a timid new-comer with infinite scorn; "hell is full of such Cliffords!" He then introduced the unfortunate man, whose name happened to be really Clifford, as "Jay-bird Charley,"—an unhallowed inspiration of the moment, that clung to him ever after.

But to return to Tennessee's Partner, whom we never knew by any other than this relative title; that he had ever existed as a separate and distinct individuality we only learned later. It seems that in 1853 he left Poker Flat to go to San Francisco, ostensibly to procure a wife. He never got any farther than Stockton. At that place he was attracted by a young person who waited upon the table at the hotel where he took his meals. One morning he said something to her which caused her to smile not unkindly, to somewhat coquettishly break a plate of toast over his up-turned, serious, simple face, and to retreat to the kitchen. He followed her, and emerged a few moments later, covered with more toast and victory. That day week they were married by a Justice of the Peace, and returned to Poker Flat. I am aware that something more might be made of this episode, but I prefer to tell it as it was current at Sandy Bar—in the

21

gulches and bar-rooms—where all sentiment was modified by a strong sense of humor.

Of their married felicity but little is known, perhaps for the reason that Tennessee, then living with his partner, one day took occasion to say something to the bride on his own account, at which, it is said, she smiled not unkindly and chastely retreated,—this time as far as Marysville, where Tennessee followed her, and where they went to housekeeping without the aid of a Justice of the Peace. Tennessee's Partner took the loss of his wife simply and seriously, as was his fashion. But to everybody's surprise, when Tennessee one day returned from Marysville, without his partner's wife,—she having smiled and retreated with somebody else,— Tennessee's Partner was the first man to shake his hand and greet him with affection. The boys who had gathered in the cañon to see the shooting were naturally indignant. Their indignation might have found vent in sarcasm but for a certain look in Tennessee's Partner's eye that indicated a lack of humorous appreciation. In fact, he was a grave man, with a steady application to practical detail which was unpleasant in a difficulty.

Meanwhile a popular feeling against Tennessee had grown up on the Bar. He was known to be a gambler; he was suspected to be a thief. In these suspicions Tennessee's Partner was equally compromised; his continued intimacy with Tennessee after the affair above quoted could only be accounted for on the hypothesis of a copartnership of crime. At last Tennessee's guilt became flagrant. One day he overtook a stranger on his way to Red Dog. The stranger afterward related that Tennessee beguiled the time with interesting anecdote and reminiscence, but illogically concluded the interview in the following words: "And now, young man, I'll trouble you for your knife, your pistols, and your money. You see your weppings might get you into trouble at Red Dog, and your money's a temptation to the evilly disposed. I think you said your address was San Francisco. I shall endeavor to call." It may be stated here that Tennessee had a fine flow of humor, which no business preoccupation could wholly subdue.

This exploit was his last. Red Dog and Sandy Bar made common cause against the highwayman. Tennessee was hunted in very much the same fashion as his prototype, the grizzly. As the toils closed around him, he made a desperate dash through the Bar, emptying his revolver at the crowd before the Arcade Saloon, and so on up Grizzly Cañon; but at its farther extremity he was stopped by a small man on a gray horse. The men looked at each other a moment in silence. Both were fearless, both self-possessed and independent; and both types of a civilization that in the seventeenth century would have been called heroic, but, in the

nineteenth, simply "reckless." "What have you got there?—I call," said
Tennessee, quietly. "Two bowers and an ace," said the stranger, as quietly,
showing two revolvers and a bowie knife. "That takes me," returned
Tennessee; and with this gambler's epigram, he threw away his useless
pistol, and rode back with his captor.

It was a warm night. The cool breeze which usually sprang up with the
going down of the sun behind the *chaparral*-crested mountain was that
evening withheld from Sandy Bar. The little cañon was stifling with
heated resinous odors, and the decaying drift-wood on the Bar sent forth
faint, sickening exhalations. The feverishness of day, and its fierce pas-
sions, still filled the camp. Lights moved restlessly along the bank of the
river, striking no answering reflection from its tawny current. Against the
blackness of the pines the windows of the old loft above the express-office
stood out staringly bright; and through their curtainless panes the
loungers below could see the forms of those who were even then deciding
the fate of Tennessee. And above all this, etched on the dark firmament,
rose the Sierra, remote and passionless, crowned with remoter passionless
stars.

The trial of Tennessee was conducted as fairly as was consistent with
a judge and jury who felt themselves to some extent obliged to justify,
in their verdict, the previous irregularities of arrest and indictment. The
law of Sandy Bar was implacable, but not vengeful. The excitement and
personal feeling of the chase were over; with Tennessee safe in their
hands they were ready to listen patiently to any defense, which they
were already satisfied was insufficient. There being no doubt in their
own minds, they were willing to give the prisoner the benefit of any that
might exist. Secure in the hypothesis that he ought to be hanged, on
general principles, they indulged him with more latitude of defense
than his reckless hardihood seemed to ask. The Judge appeared to be
more anxious than the prisoner, who, otherwise unconcerned, evidently
took a grim pleasure in the responsibility he had created. "I don't take
any hand in this yer game," had been his invariable, but good-humored
reply to all questions. The Judge—who was also his captor—for a
moment vaguely regretted that he had not shot him "on sight," that
morning, but presently dismissed this human weakness as unworthy of
the judicial mind. Nevertheless, when there was a tap at the door, and it
was said that Tennessee's Partner was there on behalf of the prisoner, he
was admitted at once without question. Perhaps the younger members
of the jury, to whom the proceedings were becoming irksomely
thoughtful, hailed him as a relief.

For he was not, certainly, an imposing figure. Short and stout, with a square face, sunburned into a preternatural redness, clad in a loose duck "jumper," and trousers streaked and splashed with red soil, his aspect under any circumstances would have been quaint, and was now even ridiculous. As he stooped to deposit at his feet a heavy carpet-bag he was carrying, it became obvious, from partially developed regions and inscriptions, that the material with which his trousers had been patched had been originally intended for a less ambitious covering. Yet he advanced with great gravity, and after having shaken the hand of each person in the room with labored cordiality, he wiped his serious, perplexed face on a red bandanna handkerchief, a shade lighter than his complexion, laid his powerful hand upon the table to steady himself, and thus addressed the Judge:—

"I was passin' by," he began, by way of apology, "and I thought I'd just step in and see how things was gittin' on with Tennessee thar—my pardner. It's a hot night. I disremember any sich weather before on the Bar."

He paused a moment, but nobody volunteering any other meteorological recollection, he again had recourse to his pocket-handkerchief, and for some moments mopped his face diligently.

"Have you anything to say in behalf of the prisoner?" said the Judge, finally.

"Thet's it," said Tennessee's Partner, in a tone of relief. "I come yar as Tennessee's pardner—knowing him nigh on four years, off and on, wet and dry, in luck and out o' luck. His ways ain't allers my ways, but thar ain't any p'ints in that young man, thar ain't any liveliness as he's been up to, as I don't know. And you sez to me, sez you—confidential-like, and between man and man—sez you, 'Do you know anything in his behalf?' and I sez to you, sez I—confidential-like, as between man and man— 'What should a man know of his pardner?' "

"Is this all you have to say?" asked the Judge, impatiently, feeling, perhaps, that a dangerous sympathy of humor was beginning to humanize the Court.

"Thet's so," continued Tennessee's Partner. "It ain't for me to say anything agin' him. And now what's the case? Here's Tennessee wants money, wants it bad, and doesn't like to ask it of his old pardner. Well, what does Tennessee do? He lays for a stranger, and he fetches that stranger. And you lays for *him*, and you fetches *him*; and the honors is easy. And I put it to you, bein' a far-minded man, and to you, gentlemen, all, as far-minded men, ef this isn't so."

"Prisoner," said the Judge, interrupting, "have you any questions to ask this man?"

"No! no!" continued Tennessee's Partner, hastily. "I play this yer hand alone. To come down to the bed-rock, it's just this: Tennessee, thar, has played it pretty rough and expensive-like on a stranger, and on this yer camp. And now, what's the fair thing? Some would say more; some would say less. Here's seventeen hundred dollars in coarse gold and a watch,— it's about all my pile,—and call it square!" And before a hand could be raised to prevent him, he had emptied the contents of the carpet-bag upon the table.

For a moment his life was in jeopardy. One or two men sprang to their feet, several hands groped for hidden weapons, and a suggestion to "throw him from the window" was only overridden by a gesture from the Judge. Tennessee laughed. And apparently oblivious of the excitement, Tennessee's Partner improved the opportunity to mop his face again with his handkerchief.

When order was restored, and the man was made to understand, by the use of forcible figures and rhetoric, that Tennessee's offense could not be condoned by money, his face took a more serious and sanguinary hue, and those who were nearest to him noticed that his rough hand trembled slightly on the table. He hesitated a moment as he slowly returned the gold to the carpet-bag, as if he had not yet entirely caught the elevated sense of justice which swayed the tribunal, and was perplexed with the belief that he had not offered enough. Then he turned to the Judge, and saying, "This yer is a lone hand, played alone, and without my pardner," he bowed to the jury and was about to withdraw, when the Judge called him back. "If you have anything to say to Tennessee, you had better say it now." For the first time that evening the eyes of the prisoner and his strange advocate met. Tennessee smiled, showed his white teeth, and saying, "Euchred, old man!" held out his hand. Tennessee's Partner took it in his own, and saying, "I just dropped in as I was passin' to see how things was gettin' on," let the hand passively fall, and adding that "it was a warm night," again mopped his face with his handkerchief, and without another word withdrew.

The two men never again met each other alive. For the unparalleled insult of a bribe offered to Judge Lynch—who, whether bigoted, weak, or narrow, was at least incorruptible—firmly fixed in the mind of that mythical personage any wavering determination of Tennessee's fate; and at the break of day he was marched, closely guarded, to meet it at the top of Marley's Hill.

How he met it, how cool he was, how he refused to say anything, how perfect were the arrangements of the committee, were all duly reported, with the addition of a warning moral and example to all future evil-doers, in the Red Dog Clarion, by its editor, who was present, and to whose vigorous English I cheerfully refer the reader. But the beauty of that midsummer morning, the blessed amity of earth and air and sky, the awakened life of the free woods and hills, the joyous renewal and promise of Nature, and above all, the infinite Serenity that thrilled through each, was not reported, as not being a part of the social lesson. And yet, when the weak and foolish deed was done, and a life, with its possibilities and responsibilities, had passed out of the misshapen thing that dangled between earth and sky, the birds sang, the flowers bloomed, the sun shone, as cheerily as before; and possibly the Red Dog Clarion was right.

Tennessee's Partner was not in the group that surrounded the ominous tree. But as they turned to disperse, attention was drawn to the singular appearance of a motionless donkey-cart halted at the side of the road. As they approached, they at once recognized the venerable "Jenny" and the two-wheeled cart as the property of Tennessee's Partner,—used by him in carrying dirt from his claim; and a few paces distant the owner of the equipage himself, sitting under a buckeye-tree, wiping the perspiration from his glowing face. In answer to an inquiry, he said he had come for the body of the "diseased" "if it was all the same to the committee." He didn't wish to "hurry anything;" he could "wait." He was not working that day; and when the gentlemen were done with the "diseased," he would take him. "Ef thar is any present," he added, in his simple, serious way, "as would care to jine in the fun'l, they kin come." Perhaps it was from a sense of humor, which I have already intimated was a feature of Sandy Bar,—perhaps it was from something even better than that; but two-thirds of the loungers accepted the invitation at once.

It was noon when the body of Tennessee was delivered into the hands of his partner. As the cart drew up to the fatal tree, we noticed that it contained a rough oblong box, apparently made from a section of sluicing,—and half filled with bark and the tassels of pine. The cart was further decorated with slips of willow, and made fragrant with buckeye-blossoms. When the body was deposited in the box, Tennessee's Partner drew over it a piece of tarred canvas, and gravely mounting the narrow seat in front, with his feet upon the shafts, urged the little donkey forward. The equipage moved slowly on, at that decorous pace which was habitual with "Jenny," even under less solemn circumstances. The men—half-curiously, half-jestingly, but all good-humoredly—strolled along beside the cart; some in advance, some a little in the rear of the homely catafalque. But, whether from the narrowing of the road or some present sense of decorum, as the cart passed on the company fell to the rear in couples, keeping step, and otherwise assuming the external show of a formal procession. Jack Folinsbee, who had at the outset played a funeral march in dumb show upon an imaginary trombone, desisted, from a lack of sympathy and appreciation,—not having, perhaps, your true humorist's capacity to be content with the enjoyment of his own fun.

The way led through Grizzly Cañon—by this time clothed in funereal drapery and shadows. The red-woods, burying their moccasined feet in the red soil, stood in Indian file along the track, trailing an uncouth benediction from their bending boughs upon the passing bier. A hare, surprised into helpless activity, sat upright and pulsating in the ferns by the roadside as the *cortége* went by. Squirrels hastened to gain a secure outlook from higher boughs; and the blue-jays, spreading their wings, fluttered before them like out-riders, until the outskirts of Sandy Bar were reached, and the solitary cabin of Tennessee's Partner.

Viewed under more favorable circumstances, it would not have been a cheerful place. The unpicturesque site, the rude and unlovely outlines, the unsavory details, which distinguish the nest-building of the California miner, were all here, with the dreariness of decay superadded. A few paces from the cabin there was a rough enclosure, which, in the brief days of Tennessee's Partner's matrimonial felicity, had been used as a garden, but was now overgrown with fern. As we approached it, we were surprised to find that what we had taken for a recent attempt at cultivation was the broken soil about an open grave.

The cart was halted before the enclosure; and rejecting the offers of assistance with the same air of simple self-reliance he had displayed throughout, Tennessee's Partner lifted the rough coffin on his back, and deposited it, unaided, within the shallow grave. He then nailed down the board which served as a lid; and mounting the little mound of earth beside it, took off his hat, and slowly mopped his face with his handkerchief. This the crowd felt was a preliminary to speech; and they disposed themselves variously on stumps and boulders, and sat expectant.

"When a man," began Tennessee's Partner, slowly, "has been running free all day, what's the natural thing for him to do? Why, to come home. And if he ain't in a condition to go home, what can his best friend do? Why, bring him home! And here's Tennessee has been running free, and we brings him home from his wandering." He paused, and picked up a fragment of quartz, rubbed it thoughtfully on his sleeve, and went on: "It ain't the first time that I've packed him on my back, as you see'd me now. It ain't the first time that I brought him to this yer cabin when he couldn't help himself; it ain't the first time that I and 'Jinny' have waited for him on yon hill, and picked him up and so fetched him home, when he couldn't speak, and didn't know me. And now that it's the last time, why——" he paused, and rubbed the quartz gently on his sleeve—"you see it's a sort of rough on his partner. And now, gentlemen," he added, abruptly, picking up his long-handled shovel, "the fun'l's over; and my thanks, and Tennessee's thanks to you for your trouble."

Resisting any proffers of assistance, he began to fill in the grave, turning his back upon the crowd, that after a few moments' hesitation gradually withdrew. As they crossed the little ridge that hid Sandy Bar from view, some, looking back, thought they could see Tennessee's Partner, his work done, sitting upon the grave, his shovel between his knees, and his face buried in his red bandanna handkerchief. But it was argued by others that you couldn't tell his face from his handkerchief at that distance; and this point remained undecided.

In the reaction that followed the feverish excitement of that day, Tennessee's Partner was not forgotten. A secret investigation had cleared him of any complicity in Tennessee's guilt, and left only a suspicion of his general sanity. Sandy Bar made a point of calling on him, and proffering various uncouth, but well-meant kindnesses. But from that day his rude health and great strength seemed visibly to decline; and when the rainy season fairly set in, and the tiny grass-blades were beginning to peep from the rocky mound above Tennessee's grave, he took to his bed.

One night, when the pines beside the cabin were swaying in the storm, and trailing their slender fingers over the roof, and the roar and rush of the swollen river were heard below, Tennessee's Partner lifted his head from the pillow, saying, "It is time to go for Tennessee; I must put 'Jinny' in the cart;" and would have risen from his bed but for the restraint of his attendant. Struggling, he still pursued his singular fancy: "There, now, steady, 'Jinny,'—steady, old girl. How dark it is! Look out for the ruts,—and look out for him, too, old gal. Sometimes, you know, when he's blind drunk, he drops down right in the trail. Keep on straight up to the pine on the top of the hill. Thar—I told you so!—thar he is,—coming this way, too,—all by himself, sober, and his face a-shining. Tennessee! Pardner!"

And so they met.

M'liss

CHAPTER I

JUST WHERE THE Sierra Nevada begins to subside in gentler undulations, and the rivers grow less rapid and yellow, on the side of a great red mountain, stands "Smith's Pocket." Seen from the red road at sunset, in the red light and the red dust, its white houses look like the outcroppings of quartz on the mountain-side. The red stage topped with red-shirted passengers is lost to view half a dozen times in the tortuous descent, turning up unexpectedly in out-of-the-way places, and vanishing altogether within a hundred yards of the town. It is probably owing to this sudden twist in the road that the advent of a stranger at Smith's Pocket is usually attended with a peculiar circumstance. Dismounting from the vehicle at the stage office, the too confident traveller is apt to walk straight out of town under the impression that it lies in quite another direction. It is related that one of the tunnel-men, two miles from town, met one of these self-reliant passengers with a carpet-bag, umbrella, Harper's Magazine, and other evidences of "Civilization and Refinement," plodding along over the road he had just ridden, vainly endeavoring to find the settlement of Smith's Pocket.

An observant traveller might have found some compensation for his disappointment in the weird aspect of that vicinity. There were huge fissures on the hillside, and displacements of the red soil, resembling more the chaos of some primary elemental upheaval than the work of man; while, half-way down, a long flume straddled its narrow body and disproportionate legs over the chasm, like an enormous fossil of some forgotten antediluvian. At every step smaller ditches crossed the road, hiding in their sallow depths unlovely streams that crept away to a clandestine union with the great yellow torrent below, and here and there were the ruins of some cabin with the chimney alone left intact and the hearthstone open to the skies.

The settlement of Smith's Pocket owed its origin to the finding of a "pocket" on its site by a veritable Smith. Five thousand dollars were taken out of it in one half-hour by Smith. Three thousand dollars were expended by Smith and others in erecting a flume and in tunnelling. And then Smith's Pocket was found to be only a pocket, and subject like other pockets to depletion. Although Smith pierced the bowels of the great red mountain, that five thousand dollars was the first and last return of his labor. The mountain grew reticent of its golden secrets, and the flume steadily ebbed away the remainder of Smith's fortune. Then Smith went into quartz-mining; then into quartz-milling; then into hydraulics and ditching, and then by easy degrees into saloon-keeping. Presently it was whispered that Smith was drinking a great deal; then it was known that Smith was a habitual drunkard, and then people began to think, as they are apt to, that he had never been anything else. But the settlement of Smith's Pocket, like that of most discoveries, was happily not dependent on the fortune of its pioneer, and other parties projected tunnels and found pockets. So Smith's Pocket became a settlement with its two fancy stores, its two hotels, its one express-office, and its two first families. Occasionally its one long straggling street was overawed by the assumption of the latest San Francisco fashions, imported per express, exclusively to the first families; making outraged Nature, in the ragged outline of her furrowed surface, look still more homely, and putting personal insult on that greater portion of the population to whom the Sabbath, with a change of linen, brought merely the necessity of cleanliness, without the luxury of adornment. Then there was a Methodist Church, and hard by a Monte Bank, and a little beyond, on the mountain-side, a graveyard; and then a little school-house.

"The Master," as he was known to his little flock, sat alone one night in the school-house, with some open copy-books before him, carefully making those bold and full characters which are supposed to combine the extremes of chirographical and moral excellence, and had got as far as "Riches are deceitful," and was elaborating the noun with an insincerity of flourish that was quite in the spirit of his text, when he heard a gentle tapping. The woodpeckers had been busy about the roof during the day, and the noise did not disturb his work. But the opening of the door, and the tapping continuing from the inside, caused him to look up. He was slightly startled by the figure of a young girl, dirty and shabbily clad. Still, her great black eyes, her coarse, uncombed, lustreless black hair falling over her sunburned face, her red arms and feet streaked with the red soil, were all familiar to him. It was Melissa Smith,—Smith's motherless child.

"What can she want here?" thought the master. Everybody knew

"M'liss," as she was called, throughout the length and height of Red Mountain. Everybody knew her as an incorrigible girl. Her fierce, ungovernable disposition, her mad freaks and lawless character, were, in their way, as proverbial as the story of her father's weaknesses, and as philosophically accepted by the townsfolk. She wrangled with and fought the school-boys with keener invective and quite as powerful arm. She followed the trails with a woodman's craft, and the master had met her before, miles away, shoeless, stockingless, and bareheaded on the mountain road. The miners' camps along the stream supplied her with subsistence during these voluntary pilgrimages, in freely offered alms. Not but that a larger protection had been previously extended to M'liss. The Rev. Joshua McSnagley, "stated" preacher, had placed her in the hotel as servant, by way of preliminary refinement, and had introduced her to his scholars at Sunday-school. But she threw plates occasionally at the landlord, and quickly retorted to the cheap witticisms of the guests, and created in the Sabbath-school a sensation that was so inimical to the orthodox dulness and placidity of that institution, that, with a decent regard for the starched frocks and unblemished morals of the two pink-and-white-faced children of the first families, the reverend gentleman had her ignominiously expelled. Such were the antecedents, and such the character of M'liss, as she stood before the master. It was shown in the ragged dress, the unkempt hair, and bleeding feet, and asked his pity. It flashed from her black, fearless eyes, and commanded his respect.

"I come here to-night," she said rapidly and boldly, keeping her hard glance on his, "because I knew you was alone. I wouldn't come here when them gals was here. I hate 'em and they hates me. That's why. You keep school, don't you? I want to be teached!"

If to the shabbiness of her apparel and uncomeliness of her tangled hair and dirty face she had added the humility of tears, the master would have extended to her the usual moiety of pity, and nothing more. But with the natural, though illogical instincts of his species, her boldness awakened in him something of that respect which all original natures pay unconsciously to one another in any grade. And he gazed at her the more fixedly as she went on still rapidly, her hand on that door-latch and her eyes on his:—

"My name's M'liss,—M'liss Smith! You can bet your life on that. My father's Old Smith,—Old Bummer Smith,—that's what's the matter with him. M'liss Smith,—and I'm coming to school."

"Well?" said the master.

Accustomed to be thwarted and opposed, often wantonly and cruelly, for no other purpose than to excite the violent impulses of her nature, the master's phlegm evidently took her by surprise. She stopped; she began to twist a lock of her hair between her fingers; and the rigid line of upper lip, drawn over the wicked little teeth, relaxed and quivered slightly. Then her eyes dropped, and something like a blush struggled up to her cheek, and tried to assert itself through the splashes of redder soil, and the sunburn of years. Suddenly she threw herself forward, calling on God to strike her dead, and fell quite weak and helpless, with her face on the master's desk, crying and sobbing as if her heart would break.

The master lifted her gently and waited for the paroxysm to pass. When with face still averted, she was repeating between her sobs the *mea culpa* of childish penitence,—that "she'd be good, she didn't mean to," &c., it came to him to ask her why she had left Sabbath-school.

Why had she left the Sabbath-school?—why? O yes. What did he (McSnagley) want to tell her she was wicked for? What did he tell her that God hated her for? If God hated her, what did she want to go to Sabbath-school for? *She* didn't want to be "beholden" to anybody who hated her.

Had she told McSnagley this?

Yes she had.

The master laughed. It was a hearty laugh, and echoed so oddly in the little school-house, and seemed so inconsistent and discordant with the sighing of the pines without, that he shortly corrected himself with a sigh. The sigh was quite as sincere in its way, however, and after a moment of serious silence he asked her about her father.

Her father? What father? Whose father? What had he ever done for her? Why did the girls hate her? Come now! what made the folks say, "Old Bummer Smith's M'liss!" when she passed? Yes; O yes. She wished he was dead,—she was dead,—everybody was dead; and her sobs broke forth anew.

The master, then leaning over her, told her as well as he could what you or I might have said after hearing such unnatural theories from childish lips; only bearing in mind perhaps better than you or I the unnatural facts of her ragged dress, her bleeding feet, and the omnipresent shadow of her drunken father. Then, raising her to her feet, he wrapped his shawl around her, and, bidding her come early in the morning, he walked with her down the road. There he bade her "good night." The moon shone brightly on the narrow path before them. He stood and watched the bent little figure as it staggered down the road, and waited until it had passed the little graveyard and reached the curve of the hill, where it turned and stood for a moment, a mere atom of suffering outlined against the far-off patient stars. Then he went back to his work. But the lines of the copy-book thereafter faded into long parallels of never-ending road, over which childish figures seemed to pass sobbing and crying into the night. Then, the little school-house seeming lonelier than before, he shut the door and went home.

The next morning M'liss came to school. Her face had been washed, and her coarse black hair bore evidence of recent struggles with the comb, in which both had evidently suffered. The old defiant look shone occasionally in her eyes, but her manner was tamer and more subdued. Then began a series of little trials and self-sacrifices, in which master and pupil bore an equal part, and which increased the confidence and sympathy between them. Although obedient under the master's eye, at times during the recess, if thwarted or stung by a fancied slight, M'liss would rage in ungovernable fury, and many a palpitating young savage, finding himself matched with his own weapons of torment, would seek the master with torn jacket and scratched face, and complaints of the dreadful M'liss. There was a serious division among the townspeople on the subject; some threatening to withdraw their children from such evil companionship, and others as warmly upholding the course of the master in his work of reclamation. Meanwhile, with a steady persistence that seemed quite astonishing to him on looking back afterward, the master drew M'liss gradually out of the shadow of her past life, as though it were but her natural progress down the narrow path on which he had set her feet the moonlit night of their first meeting. Remembering the experience of the evangelical McSnagley, he carefully avoided that Rock of Ages on which that unskilful pilot had shipwrecked her young faith. But if, in the course of her reading, she chanced to stumble upon those few words which have lifted such as she above the level of the older, the wiser, and the more prudent,—if she learned something of a faith that is symbolized by suffering, and the old light softened in her eyes, it did not take the shape of a lesson. A few of the plainer people had made up a little sum by which the ragged M'liss was enabled to assume the garments of respect and civilization; and often a rough shake of the hand, and words of homely commendation from a red-shirted and burly figure, sent a glow to the cheek of the young master, and set him to thinking if it was altogether deserved.

Three months had passed from the time of their first meeting, and the master was sitting late one evening over the moral and sententious copies, when there came a tap at the door, and again M'liss stood before him. She was neatly clad and clean-faced, and there was nothing, perhaps, but the long black hair and bright black eyes to remind him of his former apparition. "Are you busy?" she asked; "can you come with me?" And on his signifying his readiness, in her old wilful way she said, "Come, then, quick."

They passed out of the door together, and into the dark road. As they entered the town the master asked her whither she was going. She replied, "To see my father."

It was the first time he had heard her call him by that filial title, or indeed anything more than "Old Smith," or the "Old Man." It was the first time in three months that she had spoken of him at all, and the master knew she had kept resolutely aloof from him since her great change. Satisfied from her manner that it was fruitless to question her purpose, he passively followed. In out-of-the-way places, low groggeries, restaurants, and saloons; in gambling-halls and dance-houses, the master, preceded by M'liss, came and went. In the reeking smoke and blasphemous outcries of low dens, the child, holding the master's hand, stood and anxiously gazed, seemingly unconscious of all in the one absorbing nature of her pursuit. Some of the revellers, recognizing M'liss, called to the child to sing and dance for them, and would have forced liquor upon her but for the interference of the master. Others, recognizing him mutely, made way for them to pass. So an hour slipped by. Then the child whispered in his ear that there was a cabin on the other side of the creek, crossed by the long flume, where she thought he still might be. Thither they crossed,—a toilsome half-hour's walk, but in vain. They were returning by the ditch at the abutment of the flume, gazing at the lights of the town on the opposite bank, when suddenly, sharply, a quick report rang out on the clear night air. The echoes caught it, and carried it round and round Red Mountain, and set the dogs to barking all along the streams. Lights seemed to dance and move quickly on the outskirts of the town for a few moments, the stream rippled quite audibly beside them, a few stones loosened themselves from the hill-side, and splashed into the stream, a heavy wind seemed to surge the branches of the funereal pines, and then the silence seemed to fall thicker, heavier, and deadlier. The master turned towards M'liss with an unconscious gesture of protection, but the child had gone. Oppressed by a strange fear, he ran quickly down the trail to the river's bed, and, jumping from boulder to boulder, reached the base of Red Mountain and the outskirts of the village. Midway of the crossings he looked up and held his breath in awe. For high above him, on the narrow flume, he saw the fluttering little figure of his late companion crossing swiftly in the darkness.

He climbed the bank, and, guided by a few lights moving about a central point on the mountain, soon found himself breathless among a crowd of awe-stricken and sorrowful men. Out from among them the child appeared, and, taking the master's hand, led him silently before what seemed a ragged hole in the mountain. Her face was quite white, but her excited manner gone, and her look that of one to whom some long-expected event had at last happened,—an expression that, to the master in his bewilderment, seemed almost like relief. The walls of the cavern were partly propped by decaying timbers. The child pointed to what appeared to be some ragged cast-off clothes left in the hole by the late occupant. The master approached nearer with his flaming dip, and bent over them. It was Smith, already cold, with a pistol in his hand, and a bullet in his heart, lying beside his empty pocket.

CHAPTER II

The opinion which McSnagley expressed in reference to a "change of heart" supposed to be experienced by M'liss was more forcibly described in the gulches and tunnels. It was thought there that M'liss had "struck a good lead." So when there was a new grave added to the little enclosure, and at the expense of the master a little board and inscription put above it, the Red Mountain Banner came out quite handsomely, and did the fair thing to the memory of one of "our oldest Pioneers," alluding gracefully to that "bane of noble intellects," and otherwise genteelly shelving our dear brother with the past. "He leaves an only child to mourn his loss," says the Banner, "who is now an exemplary scholar, thanks to the efforts of the Rev. Mr. McSnagley." The Rev. McSnagley, in fact, made a strong point of M'liss's conversion, and indirectly attributing to the unfortunate child the suicide of her father, made affecting allusions in Sunday-school to the beneficial effects of the "silent tomb," and in this cheerful contemplation drove most of the children into speechless horror, and caused the pink-and-white scions of the first families to howl dismally and refuse to be comforted.

The long dry summer came. As each fierce day burned itself out in little whiffs of pearl-gray smoke on the mountain summits, and the upspringing breeze scattered its red embers over the landscape, the green wave which in early spring upheaved above Smith's grave grew sere, and dry, and hard. In those days the master, strolling in the little churchyard of a Sabbath afternoon, was sometimes surprised to find a few wild flowers plucked from the damp pine forest scattered there, and oftener rude wreaths hung upon the little pine cross. Most of these wreaths were formed of a sweet-scented grass, which the children loved to keep in their desks, intertwined with the plumes of the buckeye, the syringa, and the wood anemone; and here and there the master noticed the dark blue cowl of the monk's-hood, or deadly aconite. There was something in the odd association of this noxious plant with these memorials which occasioned a painful sensation to the master deeper than his esthetic sense. One day, during a long walk, in crossing a wooded ridge, he came upon M'liss in the heart of the forest, perched upon a prostrate pine, on a fantastic throne formed by the hanging plumes of lifeless branches, her lap full of grasses and pine-burrs, and crooning to herself one of the negro melodies of her younger life. Recognizing him at a distance, she made room for him on her elevated throne, and with a grave assumption of hospitality and patronage that would have been ridiculous had it not been so terribly earnest, she fed him with pine nuts and crab-apples. The master took that opportunity to point out to her the noxious and deadly qualities of the monk's-hood, whose dark blossoms he saw in her lap, and extorted from her a promise not to meddle with it as long as she remained his pupil. This done,—as the master had tested her integrity before,—he rested satisfied, and the strange feeling which had overcome him on seeing them died away.

Of the homes that were offered M'liss when her conversion became known, the master preferred that of Mrs. Morpher, a womanly and kind-hearted specimen of south-western efflorescence, known in her maidenhood as the "Per-rairie Rose." Being one of those who contend resolutely against their own natures, Mrs. Morpher, by a long series of self-sacrifices and struggles, had at last subjugated her naturally careless disposition to principles of "order," which she considered, in common with Mr. Pope, as "Heaven's first law." But she could not entirely govern the orbits of her satellites, however regular her own movements, and even her own "Jeemes" sometimes collided with her. Again her old nature asserted itself in her children. Lycurgus dipped into the cupboard "between meals," and Aristides came home from school without shoes, leaving those important articles on the threshold, for the delight of a bare-footed walk down the ditches. Octavia and Cassandra were "keerless" of their clothes. So with but one exception, however much the "Prairie Rose" might have trimmed and pruned and trained her own matured luxuriance, the little shoots came up defiantly wild and straggling. That one exception was Clytemnestra Morpher, aged fifteen. She was the realization of her mother's immaculate conception,—neat, orderly, and dull.

It was an amiable weakness of Mrs. Morpher to imagine that "Clytie" was a consolation and model for M'liss. Following this fallacy, Mrs. Morpher threw Clytie at the head of M'liss when she was "bad," and set her up before the child for adoration in her penitential moments. It was not, therefore, surprising to the master to hear that Clytie was coming to school, obviously as a favor to the master and as an example for M'liss and others. For "Clytie" was quite a young lady. Inheriting her mother's physical peculiarities, and in obedience to the climatic laws of the Red Mountain region, she was an early bloomer. The youth of "Smith's Pocket," to whom this kind of flower was rare, sighed for her in April and languished in May. Enamoured swains haunted the school-house at the hour of dismissal. A few were jealous of the master.

Perhaps it was this latter circumstance that opened the master's eyes to another. He could not help noticing that Clytie was romantic; that in school she required a great deal of attention; that her pens were uniformly bad and wanted fixing; that she usually accompanied the request with a certain expectation in her eye that was somewhat disproportionate to the quality of service she verbally required; that she sometimes allowed the curves of a round, plump white arm to rest on his when he was writing her copies; that she always blushed and flung back her blond curls when she did so. I don't remember whether I have stated that the master was a young man,—it's of little consequence, however; he had been severely educated in the school in which Clytie was taking her first lesson, and, on the whole, withstood the flexible curves and facetious glance like the fine young Spartan that he was. Perhaps an insufficient quality of food may have tended to this asceticism. He generally avoided Clytie; but one evening when she returned to the school-house after something she had forgotten, and did not find it until the master walked home with her, I hear that he endeavored to make himself particularly agreeable,—partly from the fact, I imagine, that his conduct was adding gall and bitterness to the already overcharged hearts of Clytemnestra's admirers.

The morning after this affecting episode M'liss did not come to school. Noon came, but not M'liss. Questioning Clytie on the subject, it appeared that they had left for school together, but the wilful M'liss had taken another road. The afternoon brought her not. In the evening he called on Mrs. Morpher, whose motherly heart was really alarmed. Mr. Morpher had spent all day in search of her, without discovering a trace that might lead to her discovery. Aristides was summoned as a probable accomplice, but that equitable infant succeeded in impressing the household with his innocence. Mrs. Morpher entertained a vivid impression that the child would yet be found drowned in a ditch, or, what was almost as terrible, muddied and soiled beyond the redemption of soap and water. Sick at heart, the master returned to the school-house. As he lit his lamp and seated himself at his desk, he found a note lying before him addressed to himself, in M'liss's handwriting. It seemed to be written on a leaf torn from some old memorandum-book, and to prevent sacrilegious trifling, had been sealed with six broken wafers. Opening it almost tenderly, the master read as follows:—

RESPECTED SIR,—When you read this, I am run away. Never to come back. *Never*, NEVER, NEVER. You can give my beeds to Mary Jennings, and my Amerika's Pride [a highly colored lithograph from a tobacco-box] to Sally Flanders. But don't you give anything to Clytie Morpher. Don't you dare to. Do you know what my opinion is of her, it is this, she is perfekly disgustin. That is all and no more at present from

Yours respectfully,

MELISSA SMITH.

The master sat pondering on this strange epistle till the moon lifted its bright face above the distant hills, and illuminated the trail that led to the school-house, beaten quite hard with the coming and going of little feet. Then, more satisfied in mind, he tore the missive into fragments and scattered them along the road.

At sunrise the next morning he was picking his way through the palm-like fern and thick underbrush of the pine-forest, starting the hare from its form, and awakening a querulous protest from a few dissipated crows, who had evidently been making a night of it, and so came to the wooded ridge where he had once found M'liss. There he found the prostrate pine and tasselled branches, but the throne was vacant. As he drew nearer, what might have been some frightened animal started through the crackling limbs. It ran up the tossed arms of the fallen monarch, and sheltered itself in some friendly foliage. The master, reaching the old seat, found the nest still warm; looking up in the intertwining branches, he met the black eyes of the errant M'liss. They gazed at each other without speaking. She was the first to break the silence.

"What do you want?" she asked curtly.

The master had decided on a course of action. "I want some crab-apples," he said, humbly.

"Shan't have 'em; go away. Why don't you get 'em of Clytem-nerestera?" (It seemed to be a relief to M'liss to express her contempt in additional syllables to that classical young woman's already long-drawn title.) "O you wicked thing!"

"I am hungry, Lizzy. I have eaten nothing since dinner yesterday. I am famished!" and the young man, in a state of remarkable exhaustion, leaned against the tree.

Melissa's heart was touched. In the bitter days of her gipsy life she had known the sensation he so artfully simulated. Overcome by his heart-broken tone, but not entirely divested of suspicion, she said,—

"Dig under the tree near the roots, and you'll find lots; but mind you don't tell," for M'liss had *her* hoards as well as the rats and squirrels.

But the master, of course, was unable to find them; the effects of hunger probably blinding his senses. M'liss grew uneasy. At length she peered at him through the leaves in an elfish way, and questioned,—

"If I come down and give you some, you'll promise you won't touch me?"

The master promised.

"Hope you'll die if you do!"

The master accepted instant dissolution as a forfeit. M'liss slid down the tree. For a few moments nothing transpired but the munching of the pine-nuts. "Do you feel better?" she asked, with some solicitude. The master confessed to a recuperated feeling, and then, gravely thanking her, proceeded to retrace his steps. As he expected, he had not gone far before she called him. He turned. She was standing there quite white, with tears in her widely opened orbs. The master felt that the right moment had come. Going up to her, he took both her hands, and, looking in her tearful eyes, said, gravely, "Lissy, do you remember the first evening you came to see me?"

Lissy remembered.

"You asked me if you might come to school, for you wanted to learn something and be better, and I said——"

"Come," responded the child, promptly.

"What would *you* say if the master now came to you and said that he was lonely without his little scholar, and that he wanted her to come and teach him to be better?"

The child hung her head for a few moments in silence. The master waited patiently. Tempted by the quiet, a hare ran close to the couple, and raising her bright eyes and velvet forepaws, sat and gazed at them. A squirrel ran half-way down the furrowed bark of the fallen tree, and there stopped.

"We are waiting, Lissy," said the master, in a whisper, and the child smiled. Stirred by a passing breeze, the tree-tops rocked, and a long pencil of light stole through their interlaced boughs full on the doubting face and irresolute little figure. Suddenly she took the master's hand in her quick way. What she said was scarcely audible, but the master, putting the black hair back from her forehead, kissed her; and so, hand in hand, they passed out of the damp aisles and forest odors into the open sunlit road.

Chapter III

Somewhat less spiteful in her intercourse with other scholars, M'liss still retained an offensive attitude in regard to Clytemnestra. Perhaps the jealous element was not entirely lulled in her passionate little breast. Perhaps it was only that the round curves and plump outline offered more extended pinching surface. But while such ebullitions were under the master's control, her enmity occasionally took a new and irrepressible form.

The master in his first estimate of the child's character could not conceive that she had ever possessed a doll. But the master, like many other professed readers of character, was safer in *à posteriori* than *à priori* reasoning. M'liss had a doll, but then it was emphatically M'liss's doll,— a smaller copy of herself. Its unhappy existence had been a secret discovered accidentally by Mrs. Morpher. It had been the old-time companion of M'liss's wanderings, and bore evident marks of suffering. Its original complexion was long since washed away by the weather and anointed by the slime of ditches. It looked very much as M'liss had in days past. Its one gown of faded stuff was dirty and ragged as hers had been. M'liss had never been known to apply to it any childish term of endearment. She never exhibited it in the presence of other children. It was put severely to bed in a hollow tree near the school-house, and only allowed exercise during M'liss's rambles. Fulfilling a stern duty to her doll, as she would to herself, it knew no luxuries.

Now Mrs. Morpher, obeying a commendable impulse, bought another doll and gave it to M'liss. The child received it gravely and curiously. The master, on looking at it one day, fancied he saw a slight resemblance in its round red cheeks and mild blue eyes to Clytemnestra. It became evident before long that M'liss had also noticed the same resemblance. Accordingly she hammered its waxen head on the rocks when she was alone, and sometimes dragged it with a string round its neck to and from school. At other times, setting it up on her desk, she made a pin-cushion of its patient and inoffensive body. Whether this was done in revenge of what she considered a second figurative obtrusion of Clytie's excellences upon her, or whether she had an intuitive appreciation of the rites of certain other heathens, and, indulging in that "Fetish" ceremony, imagined that the original of her wax model would pine away and finally die, is a metaphysical question I shall not now consider.

In spite of these moral vagaries, the master could not help noticing in her different tasks the working of a quick, restless, and vigorous perception. She knew neither the hesitancy nor the doubts of childhood. Her answers in class were always slightly dashed with audacity. Of course she was not infallible. But her courage and daring in passing beyond her own depth and that of the floundering little swimmers around her, in their minds outweighed all errors of judgment. Children are not better than grown people in this respect, I fancy; and whenever the little red hand flashed above her desk, there was a wondering silence, and even the master was sometimes oppressed with a doubt of his own experience and judgment.

Nevertheless, certain attributes which at first amused and entertained his fancy began to afflict him with grave doubts. He could not but see that

M'liss was revengeful, irreverent, and wilful. That there was but one better quality which pertained to her semi-savage disposition,—the faculty of physical fortitude and self-sacrifice, and another, though not always an attribute of the noble savage,—Truth. M'liss was both fearless and sincere; perhaps in such a character the adjectives were synonymous.

The master had been doing some hard thinking on this subject, and had arrived at that conclusion quite common to all who think sincerely, that he was generally the slave of his own prejudices, when he determined to call on the Rev. McSnagley for advice. This decision was somewhat humiliating to his pride, as he and McSnagley were not friends. But he thought of M'liss, and the evening of their first meeting; and perhaps with a pardonable superstition that it was not chance alone that had guided her wilful feet to the school-house, and perhaps with a complacent consciousness of the rare magnanimity of the act, he choked back his dislike and went to McSnagley.

The reverend gentleman was glad to see him. Moreover, he observed that the master was looking "peartish," and hoped he had got over the "neuralgy" and "rheumatiz." He himself had been troubled with a dumb "ager" since last conference. But he had learned to "rastle and pray."

Pausing a moment to enable the master to write his certain method of curing the dumb "ager" upon the book and volume of his brain, Mr. McSnagley proceeded to inquire after Sister Morpher. "She is an adornment to Chris*te*wanity, and has a likely growin' young family," added Mr. McSnagley; "and there's that mannerly young gal,—so well behaved,—Miss Clytie." In fact, Clytie's perfections seemed to affect him to such an extent that he dwelt for several minutes upon them. The master was doubly embarrassed. In the first place, there was an enforced contrast with poor M'liss in all this praise of Clytie. Secondly, there was something unpleasantly confidential in his tone of speaking of Mrs. Morpher's earliest born. So that the master, after a few futile efforts to say something natural, found it convenient to recall another engagement, and left without asking the information required, but in his after reflections somewhat unjustly giving the Rev. Mr. McSnagley the full benefit of having refused it.

Perhaps this rebuff placed the master and pupil once more in the close communion of old. The child seemed to notice the change in the master's manner, which had of late been constrained, and in one of their long post-prandial walks she stopped suddenly, and, mounting a stump, looked full in his face with big, searching eyes. "You ain't mad?" said she, with an interrogative shake of the black braids. "No." "Nor bothered?" "No." "Nor hungry?" (Hunger was to M'liss a sickness that might attack a person at any moment.) "No." "Nor thinking of her?" "Of whom,

Lissy?" "That white girl." (This was the latest epithet invented by M'liss, who was a very dark brunette, to express Clytemnestra.) "No." "Upon your word?" (A substitute for "Hope you'll die!" proposed by the master.) "Yes." "And sacred honor?" "Yes." Then M'liss gave him a fierce little kiss, and, hopping down, fluttered off. For two or three days after that she condescended to appear more like other children, and be, as she expressed it, "good."

Two years had passed since the master's advent at Smith's Pocket, and as his salary was not large, and the prospects of Smith's Pocket eventually becoming the capital of the State not entirely definite, he contemplated a change. He had informed the school trustees privately of his intentions, but, educated young men of unblemished moral character being scarce at that time, he consented to continue his school term through the winter to early spring. None else knew of his intention except his one friend, a Dr. Duchesne, a young Creole physician known to the people of Wingdam as "Duchesny." He never mentioned it to Mrs. Morpher, Clytie, or any of his scholars. His reticence was partly the result of a constitutional indisposition to fuss, partly a desire to be spared the questions and surmises of vulgar curiosity, and partly that he never really believed he was going to do anything before it was done.

He did not like to think of M'liss. It was a selfish instinct, perhaps, which made him try to fancy his feeling for the child was foolish, romantic, and unpractical. He even tried to imagine that she would do better under the control of an older and sterner teacher. Then she was nearly eleven, and in a few years, by the rules of Red Mountain, would be a woman. He had done his duty. After Smith's death he addressed letters to Smith's relatives, and received one answer from a sister of Melissa's mother. Thanking the master, she stated her intention of leaving the Atlantic States for California with her husband in a few months. This was a slight superstructure for the airy castle which the master pictured for M'liss's house, but it was easy to fancy that some loving sympathetic woman, with the claims of kindred, might better guide her wayward nature. Yet, when the master had read the letter, M'liss listened to it carelessly, received it submissively, and afterwards cut figures out of it with her scissors, supposed to represent Clytemnestra, labelled "the white girl," to prevent mistakes, and impaled them upon the outer walls of the school-house.

When the summer was about spent, and the last harvest had been gathered in the valleys, the master bethought him of gathering in a few ripened shoots of the young idea, and of having his Harvest-Home, or Examination. So the savants and professionals of Smith's Pocket were gathered to witness that time-honoured custom of placing timid children in a constrained position, and bullying them as in a witness-box. As usual in such cases, the most audacious and self-possessed were the lucky recipients of the honors. The reader will imagine that in the present instance M'liss and Clytie were pre-eminent, and divided public attention; M'liss with her clearness of material perception and self-reliance, Clytie with her placid self-esteem and saint-like correctness of deportment. The other little ones were timid and blundering. M'liss's readiness and brilliancy, of course, captivated the greatest number and provoked the greatest applause. M'liss's antecedents had unconsciously awakened the strongest sympathies of a class whose athletic forms were ranged against the walls, or whose handsome bearded faces looked in at the windows. But M'liss's popularity was overthrown by an unexpected circumstance.

McSnagley had invited himself, and had been going through the pleasing entertainment of frightening the more timid pupils by the vaguest and most ambiguous questions delivered in an impressive funereal tone; and M'liss had soared into Astronomy, and was tracking the course of our spotted ball through space, and keeping time with the music of the spheres, and defining the tethered orbits of the planets, when McSnagley impressively arose. "Meelissy! ye were speaking of the revolutions of this yere yearth and the move-*ments* of the sun, and I think ye said it had been a-doing of it since the creashun, eh?" M'liss nodded a scornful affirmative. "Well, war that the truth?" said McSnagley, folding his arms. "Yes," said M'liss, shutting up her little red lips tightly. The handsome outlines at the windows peered further in the school-room, and a saintly Raphael-face, with blond beard and soft blue eyes, belonging to the biggest scamp in the diggings, turned toward the child and whispered, "Stick to it, M'liss!" The reverend gentleman heaved a deep sigh, and cast a compassionate glance at the master, then at the children, and then rested his look on Clytie. That young woman softly elevated her round, white arm. Its seductive curves were enhanced by a gorgeous and massive specimen bracelet, the gift of one of her humblest worshippers, worn in honor of the occasion. There was a momentary silence. Clytie's round cheeks were very pink and soft. Clytie's big eyes were very bright and blue. Clytie's low-necked white book-muslin rested softly on Clytie's white, plump shoulders. Clytie looked at the master, and the master nodded. Then Clytie spoke softly:—

"Joshua commanded the sun to stand still, and it obeyed him!" There was a low hum of applause in the school-room, a triumphant expression on McSnagley's face, a grave shadow on the master's, and a comical look of disappointment reflected from the windows. M'liss skimmed rapidly over her Astronomy, and then shut the book with a loud snap. A groan burst from McSnagley, an expression of astonishment from the school-room, a yell from the windows, as M'liss brought her red fist down on the desk, with the emphatic declaration,

"It's a d—n lie. I don't believe it!"

CHAPTER IV

The long wet season had drawn near its close. Signs of spring were visible in the swelling buds and rushing torrents. The pine-forests exhaled the fresher spicery. The azaleas were already budding, the Ceanothus getting ready its lilac livery for spring. On the green upland which climbed Red Mountain at its southern aspect the long spike of the monk's-hood shot up from its broad-leaved stool, and once more shook its dark-blue bells. Again the billow above Smith's grave was soft and green, its crest just tossed with the foam of daisies and buttercups. The little graveyard had gathered a few new dwellers in the past year, and the mounds were placed two by two by the little paling until they reached Smith's grave, and there there was but one. General superstition had shunned it, and the plot beside Smith was vacant.

There had been several placards posted about the town, intimating that, at a certain period, a celebrated dramatic company would perform, for a few days, a series of "side-splitting" and "screaming farces;" that, alternating pleasantly with this, there would be some melodrama and a grand divertisement, which would include singing, dancing, &c. These announcements occasioned a great fluttering among the little folk, and were the theme of much excitement and great speculation among the master's scholars. The master had promised M'liss, to whom this sort of thing was sacred and rare, that she should go, and on that momentous evening the master and M'liss "assisted."

The performance was the prevalent style of heavy mediocrity; the melodrama was not bad enough to laugh at nor good enough to excite. But the master, turning wearily to the child, was astonished, and felt something like self-accusation in noticing the peculiar effect upon her excitable nature. The red blood flushed in her cheeks at each stroke of her panting little heart. Her small passionate lips were slightly parted to give vent to her hurried breath. Her widely opened lids threw up and arched her black eyebrows. She did not laugh at the dismal comicalities of the funny man, for M'liss seldom laughed. Nor was she discreetly affected to the delicate extremes of the corner of a white handkerchief, as was the tender-hearted "Clytie," who was talking with her "feller" and ogling the master at the same moment. But when the performance was over, and the green curtain fell on the little stage, M'liss drew a long deep breath, and turned to the master's grave face with a half-apologetic smile and wearied gesture. Then she said, "Now take me home!" and dropped the lids of her black eyes, as if to dwell once more in fancy on the mimic stage.

On their way to Mrs. Morpher's, the master thought proper to ridicule the whole performance. Now he shouldn't wonder if M'liss thought that the young lady who acted so beautifully was really in earnest, and in love with the gentleman who wore such fine clothes. Well, if she were in love with him, it was a very unfortunate thing! "Why?" said M'liss, with an upward sweep of the drooping lid. "Oh! well, he couldn't support his wife at his present salary, and pay so much a week for his fine clothes, and then they wouldn't receive as much wages if they were married as if they were merely lovers—that is," added the master, "if they are not already married to somebody else; but I think the husband of the pretty young countess takes the tickets at the door, or pulls up the curtain, or snuffs the candles, or does something equally refined and elegant. As to the young man with nice clothes, which are really nice now, and must cost at least two and a half or three dollars, not to speak of that mantle of red drugget which I happen to know the price of, for I bought some of it for my room once; as to this young man, Lissy, he is a pretty good fellow, and if he does drink occasionally, I don't think people ought to take advantage of it and give him black eyes and throw him in the mud. Do you? I am sure he might owe me two dollars and a half a long time, before I would throw it up in his face, as the fellow did the other night at Wingdam."

M'liss had taken his hand in both of hers and was trying to look in his eyes, which the young man kept as resolutely averted. M'liss had a faint idea of irony, indulging herself sometimes in a species of sardonic humor, which was equally visible in her actions and her speech. But the young man continued in this strain until they had reached Mrs. Morpher's, and he had deposited M'liss in her maternal charge. Waiving the invitation of Mrs. Morpher to refreshment and rest, and shading his eyes with his hand to keep out the blue-eyed Clytemnestra's siren glances, he excused himself, and went home.

For two or three days after the advent of the dramatic company, M'liss was late at school, and the master's usual Friday afternoon ramble was for once omitted, owing to the absence of his trustworthy guide. As he was putting away his books and preparing to leave the school-house, a small voice piped at his side, "Please, sir?" The master turned, and there stood Aristides Morpher.

"Well, my little man," said the master, impatiently, "what is it? quick!"

"Please, sir, me and 'Kerg' thinks that M'liss is going to run away agin."

"What's that, sir?" said the master, with that unjust testiness with which we always receive disagreeable news.

"Why, sir, she don't stay home any more, and 'Kerg' and me see her talking with one of those actor fellers, and she's with him now; and please, sir, yesterday she told 'Kerg' and me she could make a speech as well as Miss Cellerstina Montmoressy, and she spouted right off by heart," and the little fellow paused in a collapsed condition.

"What actor?" asked the master.

"Him as wears the shiny hat. And hair. And gold pin. And gold chain," said the just Aristides, putting periods for commas to eke out his breath.

The master put on his gloves and hat, feeling an unpleasant tightness in his chest and thorax, and walked out in the road. Aristides trotted along by his side, endeavoring to keep pace with his short legs to the master's strides, when the master stopped suddenly, and Aristides bumped up against him. "Where were they talking?" asked the master, as if continuing the conversation.

"At the Arcade," said Aristides.

When they reached the main street the master paused. "Run down home," said he to the boy. "If M'liss is there, come to the Arcade and tell me. If she isn't there, stay home; run!" And off trotted the short-legged Aristides.

The Arcade was just across the way—a long rambling building, containing a bar-room, billiard-room, and restaurant. As the young man crossed the plaza he noticed that two or three of the passers-by turned and looked after him. He looked at his clothes, took out his handkerchief and wiped his face, before he entered the bar-room. It contained the usual number of loungers, who stared at him as he entered. One of them looked at him so fixedly and with such a strange expression, that the master stopped and looked again, and then saw it was only his own reflection in a large mirror. This made the master think that perhaps he was a little excited, and so he took up a copy of the Red Mountain Banner from one of the tables, and tried to recover his composure by reading the column of advertisements.

He then walked through the bar-room, through the restaurant, and into the billiard-room. The child was not there. In the latter apartment a person was standing by one of the tables with a broad-brimmed glazed hat on his head. The master recognized him as the agent of the dramatic company; he had taken a dislike to him at their first meeting, from the peculiar fashion of wearing his beard and hair. Satisfied that the object of his search was not there, he turned to the man with a glazed hat. He had noticed the master, but tried that common trick of unconsciousness, in which vulgar natures always fail. Balancing a billiard cue in his hand, he pretended to play with a ball in the centre of the table. The master stood opposite to him until he raised his eyes; when their glances met, the master walked up to him.

He had intended to avoid a scene or quarrel, but when he began to speak, something kept rising in his throat and retarded his utterance, and his own voice frightened him, it sounded so distant, low, and resonant. "I understand," he began, "that Melissa Smith, an orphan, and one of my scholars, has talked with you about adopting your profession. Is that so?"

The man with the glazed hat leaned over the table, and made an imaginary shot, that sent the ball spinning round the cushions. Then walking round the table he recovered the ball, and placed it upon the spot. This duty discharged, getting ready for another shot, he said,—
"S'pose she has?"

The master choked up again, but, squeezing the cushion of the table in his gloved hand, he went on:—

"If you are a gentleman, I have only to tell you that I am her guardian, and responsible for her career. You know as well as I do the kind of life you offer her. As you may learn of any one here, I have already brought her out of an existence worse than death,—out of the streets and the contamination of vice. I am trying to do so again. Let us talk like men. She has neither father, mother, sister, or brother. Are you seeking to give her an equivalent for these?"

The man with the glazed hat examined the point of his cue, and then looked around for somebody to enjoy the joke with him.

"I know that she is a strange, wilful girl," continued the master, "but she is better than she was. I believe that I have some influence over her still. I beg and hope, therefore, that you will take no further steps in this matter, but as a man, as a gentleman, leave her to me. I am willing——"
But here something rose again in the master's throat, and the sentence remained unfinished.

The man with the glazed hat, mistaking the master's silence, raised his head with a coarse, brutal laugh, and said in a loud voice,—

"Want her yourself, do you? That cock won't fight here, young man!"

The insult was more in the tone than the words, more in the glance than tone, and more in the man's instinctive nature than all these. The best appreciable rhetoric to this kind of animal is a blow. The master felt this, and with his pent-up, nervous energy finding expression in the one act, he struck the brute full in his grinning face. The blow sent the glazed hat one way and the cue another, and tore the glove and skin from the master's hand from knuckle to joint. It opened up the corners of the fellow's mouth, and spoilt the peculiar shape of his beard for some time to come.

There was a shout, an imprecation, a scuffle, and the trampling of many feet. Then the crowd parted right and left, and two sharp quick reports followed each other in rapid succession. Then they closed again about his opponent, and the master was standing alone. He remembered picking bits of burning wadding from his coat-sleeve with his left hand. Some one was holding his other hand. Looking at it, he saw it was still bleeding from the blow, but his fingers were clenched around the handle of a glittering knife. He could not remember when or how he got it.

The man who was holding his hand was Mr. Morpher. He hurried the master to the door, but the master held back, and tried to tell him as well as he could with his parched throat about "M'liss." "It's all right, my boy," said Mr. Morpher. "She's home!" And they passed out into the street together. As they walked along Mr. Morpher said that M'liss had come running into the house a few moments before, and had dragged him out, saying that somebody was trying to kill the master at the Arcade. Wishing to be alone, the master promised Mr. Morpher that he would not seek the Agent again that night, and parted from him, taking the road toward the school-house. He was surprised in nearing it to find the door open,—still more surprised to find M'liss sitting there.

The master's nature, as I have hinted before, had, like most sensitive organizations, a selfish basis. The brutal taunt thrown out by his late adversary still rankled in his heart. It was possible, he thought, that such a construction might be put upon his affection for the child, which at best was foolish and Quixotic. Besides, had she not voluntarily abnegated his authority and affection? And what had everybody else said about her? Why should he alone combat the opinion of all, and be at last obliged tacitly to confess the truth of all they had predicted? And he had been a participant in a low bar-room fight with a common boor, and risked his life, to prove what? What had he proved? Nothing! What would the people say? What would his friends say? What would McSnagley say?

In his self-accusation the last person he should have wished to meet was M'liss. He entered the door, and, going up to his desk told the child, in a few cold words, that he was busy, and wished to be alone. As she rose he took her vacant seat, and sitting down, buried his head in his hands. When he looked up again she was still standing there. She was looking at his face with an anxious expression.

"Did you kill him?" she asked.

"No!" said the master.

"That's what I gave you the knife for!" said the child, quickly.

"Gave me the knife?" repeated the master, in bewilderment.

"Yes, gave you the knife. I was there under the bar. Saw you hit him. Saw you both fall. He dropped his old knife. I gave it to you. Why didn't you stick him?" said M'liss, rapidly, with an expressive twinkle of the black eyes and a gesture of the little red hand.

The master could only look his astonishment.

"Yes," said M'liss. "If you'd asked me, I'd told you I was off with the play-actors. Why was I off with the play-actors? Because you wouldn't tell me you was going away. I knew it. I heard you tell the Doctor so. I wasn't a-going to stay here alone with those Morphers. I'd rather die first."

With a dramatic gesture which was perfectly consistent with her character, she drew from her bosom a few limp green leaves, and, holding them out at arm's length, said in her quick vivid way, and in the queer pronunciation of her old life, which she fell into when unduly excited,—

"That's the poison plant you said would kill me. I'll go with the play-actors, or I'll eat this and die here. I don't care which. I won't stay here, where they hate and despise me! Neither would you let me, if you didn't hate and despise me too!"

The passionate little breast heaved, and two big tears peeped over the edge of M'liss's eyelids, but she whisked them away with the corner of her apron as if they had been wasps.

"If you lock me up in jail," said M'liss fiercely, "to keep me from the play-actors, I'll poison myself. Father killed himself,—why shouldn't I? You said a mouthful of that root would kill me, and I always carry it here," and she struck her breast with her clenched fist.

The master thought of the vacant plot beside Smith's grave, and of the passionate little figure before him. Seizing her hands in his and looking full into her truthful eyes, he said,—

"Lissy, will you go with *me?*"

The child put her arms around his neck, and said, joyfully, "Yes."

"But now—to-night?"

"To-night."

And, hand in hand, they passed into the road,—the narrow road that had once brought her weary feet to the master's door, and which it seemed she should not tread again alone. The stars glittered brightly above them. For good or ill the lesson had been learned, and behind them the school of Red Mountain closed upon them for ever.

An Ingénue of the Sierras

ONE

WE ALL HELD our breath as the coach rushed through the semidarkness of Galloper's Ridge. The vehicle itself was only a huge lumbering shadow; its side lights were carefully extinguished, and Yuba Bill had just politely removed from the lips of an outside passenger even the cigar with which he had been ostentatiously exhibiting his coolness. For it had been rumored that the Ramon Martinez gang of "road agents" were "laying" for us on the second grade, and would time the passage of our lights across Galloper's in order to intercept us in the "brush" beyond. If we could cross the ridge without being seen, and so get through the brush before they reached it, we were safe. If they followed, it would only be a stern chase with the odds in our favor.

The huge vehicle swayed from side to side, rolled, dipped, and plunged, but Bill kept the track, as if, in the whispered words of the expressman, he could "feel and smell" the road he could no longer see. We knew that at times we hung perilously over the edge of slopes that eventually dropped a thousand feet sheer to the tops of the sugar pines below, but we knew that Bill knew it also. The half visible heads of the horses, drawn wedgewise together by the tightened reins, appeared to cleave the darkness like a plowshare, held between his rigid hands. Even the hoofbeats of the six horses had fallen into a vague, monotonous, distant roll. Then the ridge was crossed, and we plunged into the still blacker obscurity of the brush. Rather we no longer seemed to move—it was only the phantom night that rushed by us. The horses might have been submerged in some swift Lethean stream; nothing but the top of the coach and the rigid bulk of Yuba Bill arose above them. Yet even in that awful moment our speed was unslackened; it was as if Bill cared no longer to *guide* but only to drive, or as if the direction of his huge machine was determined by other hands than his. An incautious whisperer hazarded the paralyzing suggestion of our "meeting another team." To our great astonishment Bill overheard it; to our greater astonishment he replied. "It 'ud be only a neck and neck race which would get to h—ll first," he said quietly. But we were relieved—for he had *spoken!* Almost simultaneously the wider turnpike began to glimmer faintly as a visible track before us; the wayside trees fell out of line, opened up, and dropped off one after another; we were on the broader tableland, out of danger, and apparently unperceived and unpursued.

Nevertheless in the conversation that broke out again with the relighting of the lamps, and the comments, congratulations, and reminiscences that were freely exchanged, Yuba Bill preserved a dissatisfied and even resentful silence. The most generous praise of his skill and courage awoke no response. "I reckon the old man waz just spilin' for a fight, and is feelin' disappointed," said a passenger. But those who knew that Bill had the true fighter's scorn for any purely purposeless conflict were more or less concerned and watchful of him. He would drive steadily for four or five minutes with thoughtfully knitted brows, but eyes still keenly observant under his slouched hat, and then, relaxing his strained attitude, would give way to a movement of impatience. "You ain't uneasy about anything, Bill, are you?" asked the expressman confidentially. Bill lifted his eyes with a slightly contemptuous surprise. "Not about anything ter *come*. It's what *hez* happened that I don't exackly *sabe*. I don't see no signs of Ramon's gang ever havin' been out at all, and ef they were out I don't see why they didn't go for us."

"The simple fact is that our ruse was successful," said an outside passenger. "They waited to see our lights on the ridge, and not seeing them, missed us until we had passed. That's my opinion."

"You ain't puttin' any price on that opinion, air ye?" inquired Bill politely.

"No."

" 'Cos thar's a comic paper in 'Frisco pays for them things, and I've seen worse things in it."

"Come off, Bill," retorted the passenger, slightly nettled by the tittering of his companions. "Then what did you put out the lights for?"

"Well," returned Bill grimly, "it mout have been because I didn't keer to hev you chaps blazin' away at the first bush you *thought* you saw move in your skeer, and bringin' down their fire on us."

The explanation, though unsatisfactory, was by no means an improbable one, and we thought it better to accept it with a laugh. Bill, however, resumed his abstracted manner.

"Who got in at the Summit?" he at last asked abruptly of the expressman.

"Derrick and Simpson of Cold Spring, and one of the 'Excelsior' boys," responded the expressman.

"And that Pike County girl from Dow's Flat, with her bundles. Don't forget her," added the outside passenger ironically.

"Does anybody here know her?" continued Bill, ignoring the irony.

"You'd better ask Judge Thompson; he was mighty attentive to her; gettin' her a seat by the off window, and lookin' after her bundles and things."

"Gettin' her a seat by the *window?*" repeated Bill.

"Yes, she wanted to see everything, and wasn't afraid of the shooting."

"Yes," broke in a third passenger, "and he was so d—d civil that when she dropped her ring in the straw, he struck a match agin all your rules, you know, and held it for her to find it. And it was just as we were crossin' through the brush, too. I saw the hull thing through the window, for I was hanging over the wheels with my gun ready for action. And it wasn't no fault of Judge Thompson's if his d—d foolishness hadn't shown us up, and got us a shot from the gang."

Bill gave a short grunt, but drove steadily on without further comment or even turning his eyes to the speaker.

We were now not more than a mile from the station at the crossroads where we were to change horses. The lights already glimmered in the distance, and there was a faint suggestion of the coming dawn on the summits of the ridge to the west. We had plunged into a belt of timber, when suddenly a horseman emerged at a sharp canter from a trail that seemed to be parallel with our own. We were all slightly startled, Yuba Bill alone preserving his moody calm.

"Hullo!" he said.

The stranger wheeled to our side as Bill slackened his speed. He seemed to be a "packer" or freight muleteer.

"Ye didn't get 'held up' on the Divide?" continued Bill cheerfully.

"No," returned the packer, with a laugh; "*I* don't carry treasure. But I see you're all right, too. I saw you crossin' over Galloper's."

"*Saw* us?" said Bill sharply. "We had our lights out."

"Yes, but there was suthin' white—a handkerchief or woman's veil, I reckon—hangin' from the window. It was only a movin' spot agin the hillside, but ez I was lookin' out for ye I knew it was you by that. Good night!"

He cantered away. We tried to look at each other's faces, and at Bill's expression in the darkness, but he neither spoke nor stirred until he threw down the reins when we stopped before the station. The passengers quickly descended from the roof; the expressman was about to follow, but Bill plucked his sleeve.

"I'm goin' to take a look over this yer stage and these yer passengers with ye, afore we start."

"Why, what's up?"

"Well," said Bill, slowly disengaging himself from one of his enormous gloves, "when we waltzed down into the brush up there I saw a man, ez plain ez I see you, rise up from it. I thought our time had come and the band was goin' to play, when he sorter drew back, made a sign, and we just scooted past him."

"Well?"

"Well," said Bill, "it means that this yer coach was *passed through free* tonight."

"You don't object to *that*—surely? I think we were deucedly lucky."

Bill slowly drew off his other glove. "I've been riskin' my everlastin' life on this d—d line three times a week," he said with mock humility, "and I'm allus thankful for small mercies. *But*," he added grimly, "when it comes down to being passed free by some pal of a hoss thief, and thet called a speshal Providence, *I ain't in it!* No, sir, I ain't in it!"

Two

It was with mixed emotions that the passengers heard that a delay of fifteen minutes to tighten certain screw bolts had been ordered by the autocratic Bill. Some were anxious to get their breakfast at Sugar Pine, but others were not averse to linger for the daylight that promised greater safety on the road. The expressman, knowing the real cause of Bill's delay, was nevertheless at a loss to understand the object of it. The passengers were all well-known; any idea of complicity with the road agents was wild and impossible, and even if there was a confederate of the gang among them, he would have been more likely to precipitate a robbery than to check it. Again, the discovery of such a confederate—to whom they clearly owed their safety—and his arrest would have been quite against the Californian sense of justice, if not actually illegal. It seemed evident that Bill's quixotic sense of honor was leading him astray.

The station consisted of a stable, a wagon shed, and a building containing three rooms. The first was fitted up with "bunks" or sleeping berths for the employees; the second was the kitchen; and the third and larger apartment was dining room or sitting room, and was used as general waiting room for the passengers. It was not a refreshment station, and there was no "bar." But a mysterious command from the omnipotent Bill produced a demijohn of whiskey, with which he hospitably treated the company. The seductive influence of the liquor loosened the tongue

of the gallant Judge Thompson. He admitted to having struck a match to
enable the fair Pike Countian to find her ring, which, however, proved to
have fallen in her lap. She was "a fine, healthy young woman—a type of
the Far West, sir; in fact, quite a prairie blossom! yet simple and guileless
as a child." She was on her way to Marysville, he believed, "although she
expected to meet friends—a friend, in fact—later on." It was her first visit
to a large town—in fact, any civilized center—since she crossed the
plains three years ago. Her girlish curiosity was quite touching, and her
innocence irresistible. In fact, in a country whose tendency was to
produce "frivolity and forwardness in young girls, he found her a most
interesting young person." She was even then out in the stable yard
watching the horses being harnessed, "preferring to indulge a pardonable
healthy young curiosity than to listen to the empty compliments of the
younger passengers."

The figure which Bill saw thus engaged, without being otherwise
distinguished, certainly seemed to justify the Judge's opinion. She appeared to be a well-matured country girl, whose frank gray eyes and large
laughing mouth expressed a wholesome and abiding gratification in her
life and surroundings. She was watching the replacing of luggage in the
boot. A little feminine start, as one of her own parcels was thrown
somewhat roughly on the roof, gave Bill his opportunity. "Now there," he
growled to the helper, "ye ain't carting stone! Look out, will yer! Some of
your things, miss?" he added, with gruff courtesy, turning to her. "These
yer trunks, for instance?"

She smiled a pleasant assent, and Bill, pushing aside the helper, seized
a large square trunk in his arms. But from excess of zeal, or some other
mischance, his foot slipped, and he came down heavily, striking the
corner of the trunk on the ground and loosening its hinges and fasten-
ings. It was a cheap, common-looking affair, but the accident discovered
in its yawning lid a quantity of white, lace-edged feminine apparel of an
apparently superior quality. The young lady uttered another cry and
came quickly forward, but Bill was profuse in his apologies, himself
girded the broken box with a strap, and declared his intention of having
the company "make it good" to her with a new one. Then he casually
accompanied her to the door of the waiting room, entered, made a place
for her before the fire by simply lifting the nearest and most youthful
passenger by the coat collar from the stool that he was occupying, and
having installed the lady in it, displaced another man who was standing
before the chimney, and drawing himself up to his full six feet of height
in front of her, glanced down upon his fair passenger as he took his
waybill from his pocket.

"Your name is down here as Miss Mullins?" he said.

She looked up, became suddenly aware that she and her questioner were the center of interest to the whole circle of passengers, and with a slight rise of color, returned, "Yes."

"Well, Miss Mullins, I've got a question or two to ask ye. I ask it straight out afore this crowd. It's in my rights to take ye aside and ask it—but that ain't my style; I'm no detective. I needn't ask it at all, but act as ef I knowed the answer, or I might leave it to be asked by others. Ye needn't answer it ef ye don't like; ye've got a friend over ther—Judge Thompson—who is a friend to ye, right or wrong, jest as any other man here is—as though ye'd packed your own jury. Well, the simple question I've got to ask ye is *this*: Did you signal to anybody from the coach when we passed Galloper's an hour ago?"

We all thought that Bill's courage and audacity had reached its climax here. To openly and publicly accuse a "lady" before a group of chivalrous Californians, and that lady possessing the further attractions of youth, good looks, and innocence, was little short of desperation. There was an evident movement of adhesion towards the fair stranger, a slight muttering broke out on the right, but the very boldness of the act held them in stupefied surprise. Judge Thompson, with a bland propitiatory smile began: "Really, Bill, I must protest on behalf of this young lady"—when the fair accused, raising her eyes to her accuser, to the consternation of everybody answered with the slight but convincing hesitation of conscientious truthfulness:

"*I did*."

"Ahem!" interposed the Judge hastily, "er—that is—er—you allowed your handkerchief to flutter from the window—I noticed it myself—casually—one might say even playfully—but without any particular significance."

The girl, regarding her apologist with a singular mingling of pride and impatience, returned briefly:

"I signaled."

"Who did you signal to?" asked Bill gravely.

"The young gentleman I'm going to marry."

A start, followed by a slight titter from the younger passengers, was instantly suppressed by a savage glance from Bill.

"What did you signal to him for?" he continued.

"To tell him I was here, and that it was all right," returned the young girl, with a steadily rising pride and color.

"Wot was all right?" demanded Bill.

"That I wasn't followed, and that he could meet me on the road beyond Cass's Ridge Station." She hesitated a moment, and then, with a still greater pride, in which a youthful defiance was still mingled, said:

"I've run away from home to marry him. And I mean to! No one can stop me. Dad didn't like him just because he was poor, and dad's got money. Dad wanted me to marry a man I hate, and got a lot of dresses and things to bribe me."

"And you're taking them in your trunk to the other feller?" said Bill grimly.

"Yes, he's poor," returned the girl defiantly.

"Then your father's name is Mullins?" asked Bill.

"It's not Mullins. I—I—took that name," she hesitated, with her first exhibition of self-consciousness.

"Wot *is* his name?"

"Eli Hemmings."

A smile of relief and significance went round the circle. The fame of Eli or "Skinner" Hemmings as a notorious miser and usurer had passed even beyond Galloper's Ridge.

"The step that you're taking, Miss Mullins, I need not tell you, is one of great gravity," said Judge Thompson, with a certain paternal serious-ness of manner, in which, however, we were glad to detect a glaring affectation; "and I trust that you and your affianced have fully weighed it. Far be it from me to interfere with or question the natural affections of two young people, but may I ask you what you know of the—er—young gentleman for whom you are sacrificing so much, and perhaps imperil-ing your whole future? For instance, have you known him long?"

The slightly troubled air of trying to understand—not unlike the vague wonderment of childhood—with which Miss Mullins had received the beginning of this exordium, changed to a relieved smile of comprehen-sion as she said quickly, "Oh yes, nearly a whole year."

"And," said the Judge, smiling, "has he a vocation—is he in business?"

"Oh yes," she returned; "he's a collector."

"A collector?"

"Yes; he collects bills, you know—money," she went on, with childish eagerness, "not for himself—*he* never has any money, poor Charley—but for his firm. It's dreadful hard work, too; keeps him out for days and nights, over bad roads and baddest weather. Sometimes, when he's stole over to the ranch just to see me, he's been so bad he could scarcely keep his seat in the saddle, much less stand. And he's got to take mighty big risks, too. Times the folks are cross with him and won't pay; once they shot him in the arm, and he came to me, and I helped do it up for him. But he don't mind. He's real brave—jest as brave as he's good." There was such a wholesome ring of truth in this pretty praise that we were touched in sympathy with the speaker.

"What firm does he collect for?" asked the Judge gently.

"I don't know exactly—he won't tell me; but I think it's a Spanish firm. You see—" she took us all into her confidence with a sweeping smile of innocent yet half-mischievous artfulness—"I only know because I peeped over a letter he once got from his firm, telling him he must hustle up and be ready for the road the next day; but I think the name was Martinez—yes, Ramon Martinez."

In the dead silence that ensued—a silence so profound that we could hear the horses in the distant stable yard rattling their harness—one of the younger "Excelsior" boys burst into a hysteric laugh, but the fierce eye of Yuba Bill was down upon him, and seemed to instantly stiffen him into a silent, grinning mask. The young girl, however, took no note of it. Following out, with loverlike diffusiveness, the reminiscences thus awakened, she went on:

"Yes, it's mighty hard work, but he says it's all for me, and as soon as we're married he'll quit it. He might have quit it before, but he won't take no money of me, nor what I told him I could get out of dad! That ain't his style. He's mighty proud—if he is poor—is Charley. Why, thar's all ma's money which she left me in the Savin's Bank that I wanted to draw out— for I had the right—and give it to him, but he wouldn't hear of it! Why, he wouldn't take one of the things I've got with me, if he knew it. And so he goes on ridin' and ridin', here and there and everywhere, and gettin' more and more played out and sad, and thin and pale as a spirit, and always so uneasy about his business, and startin' up at times when we're meetin' out in the South Woods or in the far clearin', and sayin': 'I must be goin' now, Polly,' and yet always tryin' to be chiffle and chipper afore me. Why, he must have rid miles and miles to have watched for me thar in the brush at the foot of Galloper's tonight, jest to see if all was safe; and Lordy! I'd have given him the signal and showed a light if I'd died for it the next minit. There! That's what I know of Charley—that's what I'm running away from home for—that's what I'm running to him for, and I don't care who knows it! And I only wish I'd done it afore—and I would—if—if—if—he'd only *asked me!* There now!" She stopped, panted, and choked. Then one of the sudden transitions of youthful emotion overtook the eager, laughing face; it clouded up with the swift change of childhood, a lightning quiver of expression broke over it, and—then came the rain!

I think this simple act completed our utter demoralization! We smiled feebly at each other with that assumption of masculine superiority which is miserably conscious of its own helplessness at such moments. We looked out of the window, blew our noses, said: "Eh—what?" and "I say," vaguely to each other, and were greatly relieved, and yet apparently astonished, when Yuba Bill, who had turned his back upon the fair speaker, and was kicking the logs in the fireplace, suddenly swept down upon us and bundled us all into the road, leaving Miss Mullins alone. Then he walked aside with Judge Thompson for a few moments; returned to us, autocratically demanded of the party a complete reticence towards Miss Mullins on the subject matter under discussion, reentered the station, reappeared with the young lady, suppressed a faint idiotic cheer which broke from us at the spectacle of her innocent face once more cleared and rosy, climbed the box, and in another moment we were under way.

"Then she don't know what her lover is yet?" asked the expressman eagerly.

"No."

"Are *you* certain it's one of the gang?"

"Can't say *for sure*. It mout be a young chap from Yolo who bucked again the tiger[1] at Sacramento, got regularly cleaned out and busted, and joined the gang for a flier. They say thar was a new hand in that job over at Keeley's—and a mighty game one, too; and ez there was some buckshot onloaded that trip, he might hev got his share, and that would tally with what the girl said about his arm. See! Ef that's the man, I've heered he was the son of some big preacher in the States, and a college sharp to boot, who ran wild in 'Frisco, and played himself for all he was worth. They're the wust kind to kick when they once get a foot over the traces. For stiddy, comf'ble kempany," added Bill reflectively, "give *me* the son of a man that was *hanged!*"

"But what are you going to do about this?"

"That depends upon the feller who comes to meet her."

"But you ain't going to try to take him? That would be playing it pretty low down on them both."

"Keep your hair on, Jimmy! The Judge and me are only going to rastle with the sperrit of that gay young galoot when he drops down for his girl—and exhort him pow'ful! Ef he allows he's convicted of sin and will find the Lord, we'll marry him and the gal offhand at the next station, and the Judge will officiate himself for nothin'. We're goin' to have this yer elopement done on the square—and our waybill clean— you bet!"

"But you don't suppose he'll trust himself in your hands?"

"Polly will signal to him that it's all square."

"Ah!" said the expressman. Nevertheless in those few moments the men seemed to have exchanged dispositions. The expressman looked doubtfully, critically, and even cynically before him. Bill's face had

[1] Gambled at faro.

relaxed, and something like a bland smile beamed across it, as he drove confidently and unhesitatingly forward.

Day, meantime, although full blown and radiant on the mountain summits around us, was yet nebulous and uncertain in the valleys into which we were plunging. Lights still glimmered in the cabins and few ranch buildings which began to indicate the thicker settlements. And the shadows were heaviest in a little copse, where a note from Judge Thompson in the coach was handed up to Yuba Bill, who at once slowly began to draw up his horses. The coach stopped finally near the junction of a small crossroad. At the same moment Miss Mullins slipped down from the vehicle, and with a parting wave of her hand to the Judge, who had assisted her from the steps, tripped down the crossroad, and disappeared in its semiobscurity. To our surprise the stage waited, Bill holding the reins listlessly in his hands. Five minutes passed—an eternity of expectation, and as there was that in Yuba Bill's face which forbade idle questioning, an aching void of silence also! This was at last broken by a strange voice from the road:

"Go on—we'll follow."

The coach started forward. Presently we heard the sound of other wheels behind us. We all craned our necks backward to get a view of the unknown, but by the growing light we could only see that we were followed at a distance by a buggy with two figures in it. Evidently Polly Mullins and her lover! We hoped that they would pass us. But the vehicle, although drawn by a fast horse, preserved its distance always, and it was plain that its driver had no desire to satisfy our curiosity. The expressman had recourse to Bill.

"Is it the man you thought of?" he asked eagerly.

"I reckon," said Bill briefly.

"But," continued the expressman, returning to his former skepticism, "what's to keep them both from levanting together now?"

Bill jerked his hand towards the boot with a grim smile.

"Their baggage."

"Oh!" said the expressman.

"Yes," continued Bill. "We'll hang on to that gal's little frills and fixin's until this yer job's settled and the ceremony's over, jest as ef we waz her own father. And, what's more, young man," he added, suddenly turning to the expressman, "*you'll* express them trunks of hers *through to Sacramento* with your kempany's labels, and hand her the receipts and checks for them so she *can get 'em there*. That'll keep *him* outer temptation and the reach o' the gang, until they get away among white men and civilization again. When your hoary-headed ole grandfather, or to speak plainer, that partikler old whiskey-soaker known as Yuba Bill, wot sits on this

box," he continued, with a diabolical wink at the expressman, "waltzes
in to pervide for a young couple jest startin' in life, thar's nothin' mean
about his style, you bet. He fills the bill every time! Speshul Providences
take a back seat when he's around."

When the station hotel and straggling settlement of Sugar Pine, now
distinct and clear in the growing light, at last rose within rifleshot on the
plateau, the buggy suddenly darted swiftly by us, so swiftly that the faces
of the two occupants were barely distinguishable as they passed, and
keeping the lead by a dozen lengths, reached the door of the hotel. The
young girl and her companion leaped down and vanished within as we
drew up. They had evidently determined to elude our curiosity, and were
successful.

But the material appetites of the passengers, sharpened by the keen
mountain air, were more potent than their curiosity, and as the breakfast
bell rang out at the moment the stage stopped, a majority of them rushed
into the dining room and scrambled for places without giving much heed
to the vanished couple or to the Judge and Yuba Bill, who had disappeared
also. The through coach to Marysville and Sacramento was likewise waiting, for Sugar Pine was the limit of Bill's ministration, and the coach which
we had just left went no farther. In the course of twenty minutes, however,
there was a slight and somewhat ceremonious bustling in the hall and on
the veranda, and Yuba Bill and the Judge reappeared. The latter was leading, with some elaboration of manner and detail, the shapely figure of Miss
Mullins, and Yuba Bill was accompanying her companion to the buggy.
We all rushed to the windows to get a good view of the mysterious stranger
and probable ex-brigand whose life was now linked with our fair fellow
passenger. I am afraid, however, that we all participated in a certain impression of disappointment and doubt. Handsome and even cultivated-
looking, he assuredly was—young and vigorous in appearance. But there
was a certain half-shamed, half-defiant suggestion in his expression, yet
coupled with a watchful, lurking uneasiness which was not pleasant and
hardly becoming in a bridegroom—and the possessor of such a bride. But
the frank, joyous, innocent face of Polly Mullins, resplendent with a simple, happy confidence, melted our hearts again, and condoned the fellow's
shortcomings. We waved our hands; I think we would have given three
rousing cheers as they drove away if the omnipotent eye of Yuba Bill had
not been upon us. It was well, for the next moment we were summoned to
the presence of that soft-hearted autocrat.

We found him alone with the Judge in a private sitting room, standing
before a table on which there were a decanter and glasses. As we filed
expectantly into the room and the door closed behind us, he cast a glance
of hesitating tolerance over the group.

"Gentlemen," he said slowly, "you was all present at the beginnin' of a little game this mornin', and the Judge thar thinks that you oughter be let in at the finish. I don't see that it's any of *your* d—d business—so to speak; but ez the Judge here allows you're all in the secret, I've called you in to take a partin' drink to the health of Mr. and Mrs. Charley Byng—ez is now comf'ably off on their bridal tower. What *you* know or what *you* suspects of the young galoot that's married the gal ain't worth shucks to anybody, and I wouldn't give it to a yaller pup to play with, but the Judge thinks you ought all to promise right here that you'll keep it dark. That's his opinion. Ez far as my opinion goes, gen'l'men," continued Bill, with greater blandness and apparent cordiality, "I wanter simply remark, in a keerless, offhand gin'ral way, that ef I ketch any God-forsaken, lop-eared, chuckle-headed blatherin' idjet airin' *his* opinion—"

"One moment, Bill," interposed Judge Thompson with a grave smile; "let me explain. You understand, gentlemen," he said, turning to us, "the singular, and I may say affecting, situation which our good-hearted friend here has done so much to bring to what we hope will be a happy termination. I want to give here, as my professional opinion, that there is nothing in his request which, in your capacity as good citizens and law-abiding men, you may not grant. I want to tell you, also, that you are condoning no offense against the statutes; that there is not a particle of legal evidence before us of the criminal antecedents of Mr. Charles Byng, except that which has been told you by the innocent lips of his betrothed, which the law of the land has now sealed forever in the mouth of his wife, and that our own actual experience of his acts has been in the main exculpatory of any previous irregularity—if not incompatible with it. Briefly, no judge would charge, no jury convict, on such evidence. When I add that the young girl is of legal age, that there is no evidence of any previous undue influence, but rather of the reverse, on the part of the bridegroom, and that I was content, as a magistrate, to perform the ceremony, I think you will be satisfied to give your promise, for the sake of the bride, and drink a happy life to them both."

I need not say that we did this cheerfully, and even extorted from Bill a grunt of satisfaction. The majority of the company, however, who were going with the through coach to Sacramento, then took their leave, and as we accompanied them to the veranda, we could see that Miss Polly Mullins's trunks were already transferred to the other vehicle under the protecting seals and labels of the all-potent Express Company. Then the whip cracked, the coach rolled away, and the last traces of the adventurous young couple disappeared in the hanging red dust of its wheels.

But Yuba Bill's grim satisfaction at the happy issue of the episode seemed to suffer no abatement. He even exceeded his usual deliberately regulated potations, and standing comfortably with his back to the center of the now deserted bar-room, was more than usually loquacious with the expressman. "You see," he said, in bland reminiscence, "when your old Uncle Bill takes hold of a job like this, he puts it straight through without changin' hosses. Yet thar was a moment, young feller, when I thought I was stompt! It was when we'd made up our mind to make that chap tell the gal fust all what he was! Ef she'd rared or kicked in the traces, or hung back only ez much ez that, we'd hev given him jest five minits' law to get up and get and leave her, and we'd hev toted that gal and her fixin's back to her dad again! But she jest gave a little scream and start, and then went off inter hysterics, right on his buzzum, laughin' and cryin' and sayin' that nothin' should part 'em. Gosh! if I didn't think *he* woz more cut up than she about it; a minit it looked as ef *he* didn't allow to marry her arter all, but that passed, and they was married hard and fast—you bet! I reckon he's had enough of stayin' out o' nights to last him, and ef the valley settlements hevn't got hold of a very shinin' member, at least the foothills hev got shut of one more of the Ramon Martinez gang."

"What's that about the Ramon Martinez gang?" said a quiet potential voice.

Bill turned quickly. It was the voice of the Divisional Superintendent of the Express Company—a man of eccentric determination of character, and one of the few whom the autocratic Bill recognized as an equal—who had just entered the barroom. His dusty pongee cloak and soft hat indicated that he had that morning arrived on a round of inspection.

"Don't care if I do, Bill," he continued, in response to Bill's invitatory gesture, walking to the bar. "It's a little raw out on the road. Well, what were you saying about Ramon Martinez gang? You haven't come across one of 'em, have you?"

"No," said Bill, with a slight blinking of his eye, as he ostentatiously lifted his glass to the light.

"And you *won't*," added the Superintendent, leisurely sipping his liquor. "For the fact is, the gang is about played out. Not from want of a job now and then, but from the difficulty of disposing of the results of their work. Since the new instructions to the agents to identify and trace all dust and bullion offered to them went into force, you see, they can't get rid of their swag. All the gang are spotted at the offices, and it costs too much for them to pay a fence or a middleman of any standing. Why, all that flaky river gold they took from the Excelsior Company can be identified as easy as if it was stamped with the company's mark. They can't melt it down themselves; they can't get others to do it for them; they can't ship it to the mint or assay offices in Marysville and 'Frisco, for they won't take it without our certificate and seals; and *we* don't take any undeclared freight *within* the lines that we've drawn around their beat, except from people and agents known. Why, *you* know that well enough, Jim," he said, suddenly appealing to the expressman, "don't you?"

Possibly the suddenness of the appeal caused the expressman to swallow his liquor the wrong way, for he was overtaken with a fit of coughing, and stammered hastily as he laid down his glass, "Yes—of course—certainly."

"No, sir," resumed the Superintendent cheerfully, "they're pretty well played out. And the best proof of it is that they've lately been robbing ordinary passengers' trunks. There was a freight wagon 'held up' near Dow's Flat the other day, and a lot of baggage gone through. I had to go down there to look into it. Darned if they hadn't lifted a lot o' woman's wedding things from that rich couple who got married the other day out at Marysville. Looks as if they were playing it rather low-down, don't it? Coming down to hardpan and the bedrock—eh?"

The expressman's face was turned anxiously towards Bill, who, after a hurried gulp of his remaining liquor, still stood staring at the window. Then he slowly drew on one of his large gloves. "Ye didn't," he said, with a slow, drawling, but perfectly distinct, articulation, "happen to know old 'Skinner' Hemmings when you were over there?"

"Yes."

"And his daughter?"

"He hasn't got any."

"A sort o' mild, innocent, guileless child of nature?" persisted Bill, with a yellow face, a deadly calm, and Satanic deliberation.

"No. I tell you he *hasn't* any daughter. Old man Hemmings is a confirmed old bachelor. He's too mean to support more than one."

"And you didn't happen to know any o' that gang, did ye?" continued Bill, with infinite protraction.

"Yes. Knew 'em all. There was French Pete, Cherokee Bob, Kanaka Joe, One-eyed Stillson, Softy Brown, Spanish Jack, and two or three Greasers."

"And ye didn't know a man by the name of Charley Byng?"

"No," returned the Superintendent, with a slight suggestion of weariness and a distraught glance towards the door.

"A dark, stylish chap, with shifty black eyes and a curled-up merstache?" continued Bill, with dry, colorless persistence.

"No. Look here, Bill, I'm in a little bit of a hurry—but I suppose you must have your little joke before we part. Now, what *is* your little game?"

"Wot you mean?" demanded Bill, with sudden brusqueness.

"Mean? Well, old man, you know as well as I do. You're giving me the very description of Ramon Martinez himself, ha! ha! No—Bill! you didn't play me this time. You're mighty spry and clever, but you didn't catch on just then."

He nodded and moved away with a light laugh. Bill turned a stony face to the expressman. Suddenly a gleam of mirth came into his gloomy eyes. He bent over the young man, and said in a hoarse, chuckling whisper:

"But I got even after all!"

"How?"

"He's tied up to that lying little she-devil, hard and fast!"

A Protégée of Jack Hamlin's

ONE

THE STEAMER SILVEROPOLIS was sharply and steadily cleaving the broad, placid shallows of the Sacramento River. A large wave like an eagre, diverging from its bow, was extending to either bank, swamping the tules and threatening to submerge the lower levees. The great boat itself—a vast but delicate structure of airy stories, hanging galleries, fragile colonnades, gilded cornices, and resplendent frescoes—was throbbing throughout its whole perilous length with the pulse of high pressure and the strong monotonous beat of a powerful piston. Floods of foam pouring from the high paddle boxes on either side and reuniting in the wake of the boat left behind a track of dazzling whiteness, over which trailed two dense black banners flung from its lofty smokestacks.

Mr. Jack Hamlin had quietly emerged from his stateroom on deck and was looking over the guards. His hands were resting lightly on his hips over the delicate curves of his white waistcoat, and he was whistling softly, possibly some air to which he had made certain card-playing passengers dance the night before. He was in comfortable case, and his soft brown eyes under their long lashes were veiled with gentle tolerance of all things. He glanced lazily along the empty hurricane deck forward; he glanced lazily down to the saloon deck below him. Far out against the guards below him leaned a young girl. Mr. Hamlin knitted his brows slightly.

He remembered her at once. She had come on board that morning with one Ned Stratton, a brother gambler, but neither a favorite nor intimate of Jack's. From certain indications in the pair, Jack had inferred that she was some foolish or reckless creature whom "Ed" had "got on a string," and was spiriting away from her friends and family. With the abstract morality of this situation Jack was not in the least concerned. For himself he did not indulge in that sort of game; the inexperience and

67

vacillations of innocence were apt to be bothersome, and besides, a certain modest doubt of his own competency to make an original selection had always made him prefer to confine his gallantries to the wives of men of greater judgment than himself who had. But it suddenly occurred to him that he had seen Stratton quickly slip off the boat at the last landing stage. Ah! that was it; he had cast away and deserted her. It was an old story. Jack smiled. But he was not greatly amused with Stratton.

She was very pale, and seemed to be clinging to the network railing, as if to support herself, although she was gazing fixedly at the yellow glancing current below, which seemed to be sucked down and swallowed in the paddle box as the boat swept on. It certainly was a fascinating sight—this sloping rapid, hurrying on to bury itself under the crushing wheels. For a brief moment Jack saw how they would seize anything floating on that ghastly incline, whirl it round in one awful revolution of the beating paddles, and then bury it, broken and shattered out of all recognition, deep in the muddy undercurrent of the stream behind them.

She moved away presently with an odd, stiff step, chafing her gloved hands together as if they had become stiffened, too, in her rigid grasp of the railing. Jack leisurely watched her as she moved along the narrow strip of deck. She was not at all to his taste—a rather plump girl with a rustic manner and a great deal of brown hair under her straw hat. She might have looked better had she not been so haggard. When she reached the door of the saloon she paused, and then, turning suddenly, began to walk quickly back again. As she neared the spot where she had been standing her pace slackened, and when she reached the railing she seemed to relapse against it in her former helpless fashion. Jack became lazily interested. Suddenly she lifted her head and cast a quick glance around and above her. In that momentary lifting of her face Jack saw her expression. Whatever it was, his own changed instantly; the next moment there was a crash on the lower deck. It was Jack who had swung himself over the rail and dropped ten feet, to her side. But not before she had placed one foot in the meshes of the netting and had gripped the railing for a spring.

The noise of Jack's fall might have seemed to her bewildered fancy as a part of her frantic act, for she fell forward vacantly on the railing. But by this time Jack had grasped her arm as if to help himself to his feet.

"I might have killed myself by that foolin', mightn't I?" he said cheerfully.

The sound of a voice so near her seemed to recall to her dazed sense the uncompleted action his fall had arrested. She made a convulsive bound towards the railing, but Jack held her fast.

"Don't," he said in a low voice—"don't, it won't pay. It's the sickest game that ever was played by man or woman. Come here!"

He drew her towards an empty stateroom whose door was swinging on its hinges a few feet from them. She was trembling violently; he half led, half pushed her into the room, closed the door, and stood with his back against it as she dropped into a chair. She looked at him vacantly; the agitation she was undergoing inwardly had left her no sense of outward perception.

"You know Stratton would be awfully riled," continued Jack easily. "He's just stepped out to see a friend and got left by the fool boat. He'll be along by the next steamer, and you're bound to meet him in Sacramento."

Her staring eyes seemed suddenly to grasp his meaning. But to his surprise she burst out with a certain hysterical desperation, "No! no! Never! *never* again! Let me pass! I must go," and struggled to regain the door. Jack, albeit singularly relieved to know that she shared his private sentiments regarding Stratton, nevertheless resisted her. Whereat she suddenly turned white, reeled back, and sank in a dead faint in the chair.

The gambler turned, drew the key from the inside of the door, passed out, locking it behind him, and walked leisurely into the main saloon.

"Mrs. Johnson," he said gravely, addressing the stewardess, a tall mulatto, with his usual winsome supremacy over dependents and children, "you'll oblige me if you'll corral a few smelling salts, vinaigrettes, hairpins, and violet powder, and unload them in deck stateroom No. 257. There's a lady—"

"A lady, Marse Hamlin?" interrupted the mulatto, with an archly significant flash of her white teeth.

"A lady," continued Jack with unabashed gravity, "in a sort of conniption fit. A relative of mine; in fact, a niece, my only sister's child. Hadn't seen each other for ten years, and it was too much for her."

The woman glanced at him with a mingling of incredulous belief but delighted obedience, hurriedly gathered a few articles from her cabin, and followed him to No. 257. The young girl was still unconscious. The stewardess applied a few restoratives with the skill of long experience, and the young girl opened her eyes. They turned vacantly from the stewardess to Jack with a look of half recognition and half frightened inquiry.

"Yes," said Jack, addressing the eyes, although ostentatiously speaking to Mrs. Johnson, "she'd only just come by steamer to 'Frisco and wasn't expecting to see me, and we dropped right into each other here on the boat. And I haven't seen her since she was so high. Sister Mary ought to have warned me by letter; but she was always a slouch at letter writing. There, that'll do, Mrs. Johnson. She's coming round; I reckon I can manage the rest. But you go now and tell the purser I want one of those inside staterooms for my niece—*my niece*, you hear—so that you can be near her and look after her."

As the stewardess turned obediently away the young girl attempted to rise, but Jack checked her.

"No," he said, almost brusquely; "you and I have some talking to do before she gets back, and we've no time for foolin'. You heard what I told her just now! Well, it's got to be as I said, you sabe. As long as you're on this boat you're my niece, and my sister Mary's child. As I haven't got any sister Mary, you don't run any risk of falling foul of her, and you ain't taking anyone's place. That settles that. Now, do you or do you not want to see that man again? Say yes, and if he's anywhere above ground I'll yank him over to you as soon as we touch shore." He had no idea of interfering with his colleague's amours, but he had determined to make Stratton pay for the bother their slovenly sequence had caused him. Yet he was relieved and astonished by her frantic gesture of indignation and abhorrence. "No?" he repeated grimly. "Well, that settles that. Now, look here; quick, before she comes—do you want to go back home to your friends?"

But here occurred what he had dreaded most and probably thought he had escaped. She had stared at him, at the stewardess, at the walls, with abstracted, vacant, and bewildered, but always undimmed and unmoistened eyes. A sudden convulsion shook her whole frame, her blank expression broke like a shattered mirror, she threw her hands over her eyes, and fell forward with her face to the back of her chair in an outburst of tears.

Alas for Jack! with the breaking up of those sealed fountains came her speech also, at first disconnected and incoherent, and then despairing and passionate. No! she had no longer friends or home! She had lost and disgraced them! She had disgraced *herself*! There was no home for her but the grave. Why had Jack snatched her from it? Then bit by bit, she yielded up her story—a story decidedly commonplace to Jack, uninteresting, and even irritating to his fastidiousness. She was a schoolgirl (not even a convent girl, but the inmate of a Presbyterian female academy at Napa. Jack shuddered as he remembered to have once seen certain of the pupils walking with a teacher), and she lived with her married sister. She had seen Stratton while going to-and-fro on the San Francisco boat; she had exchanged notes with him, had met him secretly, and finally consented to elope with him to Sacramento, only to discover when the boat had left the wharf the real nature of his intentions. Jack listened with infinite weariness and inward chafing. He had read all this before in cheap novelettes, in the police reports, in the Sunday papers; he had heard a street preacher declaim against it, and warn young women of the serpentlike wiles of tempters of the Stratton variety. But even now Jack failed to recognize Stratton as a serpent, or indeed anything but a blundering cheat and clown, who had left his dirty 'prentice work on his (Jack's) hands. But the girl was helpless and, it seemed, homeless, all through a certain desperation of feeling which, in spite of her tears, he could not but respect. That momentary shadow of death had exalted her. He stroked his mustache, pulled down his white waistcoat, and let her cry, without saying anything. He did not know that this most objectionable phase of her misery was her salvation and his own.

But the stewardess would return in a moment.

"You'd better tell me what to call you," he said quietly. "I ought to know my niece's first name."

The girl caught her breath, and between two sobs said, "Sophonisba."

Jack winced. It seemed only to need this last sentimental touch to complete the idiotic situation.

"I'll call you Sophy," he said hurriedly and with an effort. "And now look here! You are going in that cabin with Mrs. Johnson where she can look after you, but I can't. So I'll have to take your word, for I'm not going to give you away before Mrs. Johnson, that you won't try that foolishness—you know what I mean—before I see you again. Can I trust you?"

With her head still bowed over the chair back, she murmured slowly somewhere from under her disheveled hair: "Yes."

"Honest Injin?" adjured Jack gravely.

"Yes."

The shuffling step of the stewardess was heard slowly approaching.

"Yes," continued Jack abruptly, slightly lifting his voice, as Mrs. Johnson opened the door—"yes, if you'd only had some of those spearmint drops of your aunt Rachel's that she always gave you when these fits came on you'd have been all right inside of five minutes. Aunty was no slouch of a doctor, was she? Dear me, it only seems yesterday since I saw her. You were just playing round her knee like a kitten on the back porch. How time does fly! But here's Mrs. Johnson coming to take you in. Now rouse up, Sophy, and just hook yourself on to Mrs. Johnson on that side, and we'll toddle along."

The young girl put back her heavy hair, and with her face still averted submitted to be helped to her feet by the kindly stewardess. Perhaps something homely sympathetic and nurselike in the touch of the mulatto gave her assurance and confidence, for her head lapsed quite naturally against the woman's shoulder, and her face was partly hidden as she moved slowly along the deck. Jack accompanied them to the saloon and the inner stateroom door. A few passengers gathered curiously near, as much attracted by the unusual presence of Jack Hamlin in such a procession as by the girl herself.

"You'll look after her specially, Mrs. Johnson," said Jack, in unusually deliberate terms. "She's been a good deal petted at home, and my sister perhaps has rather spoilt her. She's pretty much of a child still, and you'll have to humor her. Sophy," he continued, with ostentatious playfulness, directing his voice into the dim recesses of the stateroom, "you'll just think Mrs. Johnson's your old nurse, won't you? Think it's old Katy, hey?"

To his great consternation the girl approached tremblingly from the inner shadow. The faintest and saddest of smiles for a moment played around the corners of her drawn mouth and tear-dimmed eyes as she held out her hand and said:

"God bless you for being so kind."

Jack shuddered and glanced quickly round. But luckily no one heard this crushing sentimentalism, and the next moment the door closed upon her and Mrs. Johnson.

It was past midnight, and the moon was riding high over the narrowing yellow river, when Jack again stepped out on deck. He had just left the captain's cabin, and a small social game with the officers, which had served to some extent to vaguely relieve his irritation and their pockets. He had presumably quite forgotten the incident of the afternoon, as he looked about him, and complacently took in the quiet beauty of the night.

The low banks on either side offered no break to the uninterrupted level of the landscape, through which the river seemed to wind only as a race track for the rushing boat. Every fiber of her vast but fragile bulk quivered under the goad of her powerful engines. There was no other movement but hers, no other sound but this monstrous beat and panting; the whole tranquil landscape seemed to breathe and pulsate with her; dwellers in the tules, miles away, heard and felt her as she passed, and it seemed to Jack, leaning over the railing, as if the whole river swept like a sluice through her paddle boxes.

Jack had quite unconsciously lounged before that part of the railing where the young girl had leaned a few hours ago. As he looked down upon the streaming yellow millrace below him he noticed—what neither he nor the girl had probably noticed before—that a space of the top bar of the railing was hinged, and could be lifted by withdrawing a small bolt, thus giving easy access to the guards. He was still looking at it, whistling softly, when footsteps approached.

"Jack," said a lazy voice, "how's sister Mary?"

"It's a long time since you've seen her only child, Jack, ain't it?" said a second voice; "and yet it sort o' seems to me somehow that I've seen her before."

Jack recognized the voice of two of his late companions at the card table. His whistling ceased; so also dropped every trace of color and expression from his handsome face. But he did not turn, and remained quietly gazing at the water.

"Aunt Rachel, too, must be getting on in years, Jack," continued the first speaker, halting behind Jack.

"And Mrs. Johnson does not look so much like Sophy's old nurse as she used to," remarked the second, following his example. Still Jack remained unmoved.

"You don't seem to be interested, Jack," continued the first speaker. "What are you looking at?"

Without turning his head the gambler replied, "Looking at the boat; she's booming along, just chawing up and spitting out the river, ain't she? Look at that sweep of water going under her paddle wheels," he continued, unbolting the rail and lifting it to allow the two men to peer curiously over the guards as he pointed to the murderous incline beneath them; "a man wouldn't stand much show who got dropped into it. How these paddles would just snatch him bald-headed, pick him up, and slosh him round and round, and then sling him out down there in such a shape that his own father wouldn't know him."

"Yes," said the first speaker, with an ostentatious little laugh, "but all that ain't telling us how sister Mary is."

"No," said the gambler, slipping into the opening with a white and rigid face in which nothing seemed living but the eyes—"no; but it's telling you how two d—d fools who didn't know when to shut their mouths might get them shut once and forever. It's telling you what might happen to two men who tried to 'play' a man who didn't care to be 'played,'—a man who didn't care much what he did, when he did it, or how he did it, but would do what he'd set out to do—even if in doing it he went to hell with the men he sent there."

He had stepped out on the guards, beside the two men, closing the rail behind him. He had placed his hands on their shoulders; they had both gripped his arms; yet, viewed from the deck above, they seemed at that moment an amicable, even fraternal group, albeit the faces of the three were dead white in the moonlight.

"I don't think I'm so very much interested in sister Mary," said the first speaker quietly, after a pause.

"And I don't seem to think so much of aunt Rachel as I did," said his companion.

"I thought you wouldn't," said Jack, coolly reopening the rail and stepping back again. "It all depends upon the way you look at those things. Good night."

"Good night."

The three men paused, shook each other's hands silently, and separated, Jack sauntering slowly back to his stateroom.

Two

The educational establishment of Mrs. Mix and Madame Bance, situated in the best quarter of Sacramento and patronized by the highest state officials and members of the clergy, was a pretty if not an imposing edifice. Although surrounded by a high white picket fence and entered through a heavily boarded gate, its balconies festooned with jasmine and roses, and its spotlessly draped windows as often graced with fresh, flowerlike faces, were still plainly and provokingly visible above the ostentatious spikes of the pickets. Nevertheless, Mr. Jack Hamlin, who had six months before placed his niece, Miss Sophonisba Brown, under its protecting care, felt a degree of uneasiness, even bordering on timidity, which was new to that usually self-confident man. Remembering how his first appearance had fluttered this dovecot and awakened a severe suspicion in the minds of the two principals, he had discarded his usual fashionable attire and elegantly fitting garments for a rough homespun suit, supposed to represent a homely agriculturist, but which had the effect of transforming him into an adorable Strephon, infinitely more dangerous in his rustic shepherdlike simplicity. He had also shaved off his silken mustache for the same prudential reasons, but had only succeeded in uncovering the delicate lines of his handsome mouth, and so absurdly reducing his apparent years that his avuncular pretensions seemed more preposterous than ever; and when he had rung the bell and was admitted by a severe Irish waiting maid, his momentary hesitation and half-humorous diffidence had such an unexpected effect upon her that it seemed doubtful if he would be allowed to pass beyond the vestibule.

"Shure, miss," she said in a whisper to an underteacher, "there's wan at the dhure who calls himself 'Mister' Hamlin, but av it is not a young lady maskeradin' in her brother's clothes oim very much mistaken; and av it's a boy, one of the pupil's brothers, shure ye might put a dhress on him when you take the others out for a walk, and he'd pass for the beauty of the whole school."

Meantime the unconscious subject of this criticism was pacing somewhat uneasily up and down the formal reception room into which he had been finally ushered. Its farther end was filled by an enormous parlor organ, a number of music books, and a cheerfully variegated globe. A large presentation Bible, an equally massive illustrated volume on the Holy Land, a few landscapes in cold, bluish milk and water colors, and rigid heads in crayons—the work of pupils—were presumably ornamental. An imposing mahogany sofa and what seemed to be a disproportionate excess of chairs somewhat coldly furnished the room. Jack had reluctantly made up his mind that if Sophy was accompanied by anyone he would be obliged to kiss her to keep up his assumed relationship. As she entered the room with Miss Mix, Jack advanced and soberly saluted her on the cheek. But so positive and apparent was the gallantry of his presence, and perhaps so suggestive of some pastoral flirtation, that Miss Mix, to Jack's surprise, winced perceptibly and became stony. But he was still more surprised that the young lady herself shrank half uneasily from his lips, and uttered a slight exclamation. It was a new experience to Mr. Hamlin.

But this somewhat mollified Miss Mix, and she slightly relaxed her austerity. She was glad to be able to give the best accounts of Miss Brown, not only as regarded her studies, but as to her conduct and deportment. Really, with the present freedom of manners and laxity of home discipline in California, it was gratifying to meet a young lady who seemed to value the importance of a proper decorum and behavior, especially towards the opposite sex. Mr. Hamlin, although her guardian, was perhaps too young to understand and appreciate this. To this inexperience she must also attribute the indiscretion of his calling during school hours and without preliminary warning. She trusted, however, that this informality could be overlooked after consultation with Madame Bance, but in the meantime, perhaps for half an hour, she must withdraw Miss Brown and return with her to the class. Mr. Hamlin could wait in this public room, reserved especially for visitors, until they returned. Or, if he cared to accompany one of the teachers in a formal inspection of the school, she added doubtfully, with a glance at Jack's distracting attractions, she would submit this also to Madame Bance.

"Thank you, thank you," returned Jack hurriedly, as a depressing vision of the fifty or sixty scholars rose before his eyes, "but I'd rather not. I mean, you know, I'd just as lief stay here *alone*. I wouldn't have called anyway, don't you see, only I had a day off—and—and—I wanted to talk with my niece on family matters."

He did not say that he had received a somewhat distressful letter from her asking him to come; a new instinct made him cautious.

Considerably relieved by Jack's unexpected abstention, which seemed to spare her pupils the distraction of his graces, Miss Mix smiled more amicably and retired with her charge. In the single glance he had exchanged with Sophy he saw that, although resigned and apparently self-controlled, she still appeared thoughtful and melancholy. She had improved in appearance and seemed more refined and less rustic in her school dress, but he was conscious of the same distinct separation of her personality (which was uninteresting to him) from the sentiment that had impelled him to visit her. She was possibly still hankering after that fellow Stratton, in spite of her protestations to the contrary; perhaps she wanted to go back to her sister, although she had declared she would die first, and had always refused to disclose her real name or give any clue by which he could have traced her relations. She would cry, of course; he almost hoped that she would not return alone; he half regretted he had come. She still held him only by a single quality of her nature—the desperation she had shown on the boat; that was something he understood and respected.

He walked discontentedly to the window and looked out; he walked discontentedly to the end of the room and stopped before the organ. It was a fine instrument; he could see that with an admiring and experienced eye. He was alone in the room; in fact, quite alone in that part of the house which was separated from the classrooms. He would disturb no one by trying it. And if he did, what then? He smiled a little recklessly, slowly pulled off his gloves, and sat down before it.

He played cautiously at first, with the soft pedal down. The instrument had never known a strong masculine hand before, having been fumbled and frivoled over by softly incompetent, feminine fingers. But presently it began to thrill under the passionate hand of its lover, and carried away by his one innocent weakness, Jack was launched upon a sea of musical reminiscences. Scraps of church music, Puritan psalms of his boyhood, dying strains from sad, forgotten operas, fragments of oratorios and symphonies, but chiefly phrases from old masses heard at the missions of San Pedro and Santa Isabel, swelled up from his loving and masterful fingers. He had finished an Agnus Dei; the formal room was pulsating with divine aspiration; the rascal's hands were resting listlessly on the keys, his brown lashes lifted, in an effort of memory, tenderly towards the ceiling.

Suddenly, a subdued murmur of applause and a slight rustle behind him recalled him to himself again. He wheeled his chair quickly round. The two principals of the school and half a dozen teachers were standing gravely behind him, and at the open door a dozen curled and frizzled youthful heads peered in eagerly, but half restrained by their teachers. The relaxed features and apologetic attitude of Madame Bance and Miss Mix showed that Mr. Hamlin had unconsciously achieved a triumph.

He might not have been as pleased to know that his extraordinary performance had solved a difficulty, effaced his other graces, and enabled them to place him on the moral pedestal of a mere musician, to whom these eccentricities were allowable and privileged. He shared the admiration extended by the young ladies to their music teacher, which was always understood to be a sexless enthusiasm and a contagious juvenile disorder. It was also a fine advertisement for the organ. Madame Bance smiled blandly, improved the occasion by thanking Mr. Hamlin for having given the scholars a gratuitous lesson on the capabilities of the instrument, and was glad to be able to give Miss Brown a half-holiday to spend with her accomplished relative. Miss Brown was even now upstairs putting on her hat and mantle. Jack was relieved. Sophy would not attempt to cry on the street.

Nevertheless, when they reached it and the gate closed behind them, he again became uneasy. The girl's clouded face and melancholy manner were not promising. It also occurred to him that he might meet someone who knew him and thus compromise her. This was to be avoided at all hazards. He began with forced gaiety:

"Well, now, where shall we go?"

She slightly raised her tear-dimmed eyes.

"Where you please—I don't care."

"There isn't any show going on here, is there?"

He had a vague idea of a circus or menagerie—himself behind her in the shadow of the box.

"I don't know of any."

"Or any restaurant—or cake shop?"

"There's a place where the girls go to get candy on Main Street. Some of them are there now."

Jack shuddered; this was not to be thought of.

"But where do you walk?"

"Up and down Main Street."

"Where everybody can see you?" said Jack, scandalized.

The girl nodded.

They walked on in silence for a few moments. Then a bright idea struck Mr. Hamlin. He suddenly remembered that in one of his many fits of impulsive generosity and largess he had given to an old Negro retainer—whose wife had nursed him through a dangerous illness—a house and lot on the river bank. He had been told that they had opened a small laundry or wash house. It occurred to him that a stroll there and a call upon "Uncle Hannibal and Aunt Chloe" combined the propriety and respectability due to the young person he was with, and the requisite secrecy and absence of publicity due to himself. He at once suggested it.

"You see she was a mighty good woman, and you ought to know her, for she was my old nurse"—

The girl glanced at him with a sudden impatience.

"Honest Injin," said Jack solemnly; "she did nurse me through my last cough. I ain't playing old family gags on you now."

"Oh, dear," burst out the girl impulsively, "I do wish you wouldn't ever play them again. I wish you wouldn't pretend to be my uncle; I wish you wouldn't make me pass for your niece. It isn't right. It's all wrong. Oh, don't you know it's all wrong, and can't come right any way? It's just killing me. I can't stand it. I'd rather you'd say what I am and how I came to you and how you pitied me."

They had luckily entered a narrow side street, and the sobs which shook the young girl's frame were unnoticed. For a few moments Jack felt a horrible conviction stealing over him, that in his present attitude towards her he was not unlike that hound Stratton, and that, however innocent his own intent, there was a sickening resemblance to the situation on the boat in the base advantage he had taken of her friendlessness. He had never told her that he was a gambler like Stratton, and that his peculiar infelix reputation among women made it impossible for him to assist her, except by stealth or the deception he had practiced, without compromising her. He who had for years faced the sneers and half-frightened opposition of the world dared not tell the truth to this girl, from whom he expected nothing and who did not interest him. He felt he was almost slinking at her side. At last he said desperately:

"But I snatched them bald-headed at the organ, Sophy, didn't I?"

"Oh, yes," said the girl, "you played beautifully and grandly. It was so good of you, too. For I think, somehow, Madame Bance had been a little suspicious of you, but that settled it. Everybody thought it was fine, and some thought it was your profession. Perhaps," she added timidly, "it is."

"I play a good deal, I reckon," said Jack, with a grim humor which did not, however, amuse him.

"I wish *I* could, and make money by it," said the girl eagerly. Jack winced, but she did not notice it as she went on hurriedly: "That's what I wanted to talk to you about. I want to leave the school and make my own living. Anywhere where people won't know me and where I can be alone and work. I shall die here among these girls—with all their talk of their friends and their—sisters—and their questions about you."

"Tell 'em to dry up," said Jack indignantly. "Take 'em to the cake shop and load 'em up with candy and ice cream. That'll stop their mouths. You've got money—you got my last remittance, didn't you?" he repeated quickly. "If you didn't here's—"; his hand was already in his pocket when she stopped him with a despairing gesture.

"Yes, yes, I got it all. I haven't touched it. I don't want it. For I can't live on you. Don't you understand—I want to work. Listen—I can draw and paint. Madame Bance says I do it well; my drawing master says I might in time take portraits and get paid for it. And even now I can retouch photographs and make colored miniatures from them. And," she stopped and glanced at Jack half timidly, "I've—done some already."

A glow of surprised relief suffused the gambler. Not so much at this astonishing revelation as at the change it seemed to effect in her. Her pale blue eyes, made paler by tears, cleared and brightened under their swollen lids like wiped steel; the lines of her depressed mouth straightened and became firm. Her voice had lost its hopeless monotone.

"There's a shop in the next street—a photographer's—where they have one of mine in their windows," she went on, reassured by Jack's unaffected interest. "It's only round the corner, if you care to see."

Jack assented; a few paces farther brought them to the corner of a narrow street, where they presently turned into a broader thoroughfare and stopped before the window of a photographer. Sophy pointed to an oval frame, containing a portrait painted on porcelain. Mr. Hamlin was startled. Inexperienced as he was, a certain artistic inclination told him it was good, although it is to be feared he would have been astonished even if it had been worse. The mere fact that this headstrong country girl, who had run away with a cur like Stratton, should be able to do anything else took him by surprise.

"I got ten dollars for that," she said hesitatingly, "and I could have got more for a larger one, but I had to do that in my room during recreation hours. If I had more time and a place where I could work—" She stopped timidly and looked tentatively at Jack. But he was already indulging in a characteristically reckless idea of coming back after he had left Sophy, buying the miniature at an extravagant price, and ordering half a dozen more at extraordinary figures. Here, however, two passersby, stopping ostensibly to look in the window, but really attracted by the picturesque spectacle of the handsome young rustic and his schoolgirl companion, gave Jack such a fright that he hurried Sophy away again into the side street.

"There's nothing mean about that picture business," he said cheerfully; "it looks like a square kind of game," and relapsed into thoughtful silence.

At which Sophy, the ice of restraint broken, again burst into passionate appeal. If she could only go away somewhere—where she saw no one but the people who would buy her work, who knew nothing of her past nor cared to know who were her relations! She would work hard; she knew she could support herself in time. She would keep the name he had given her—it was not distinctive enough to challenge any inquiry—but nothing more. She need not assume to be his niece; he would always be her kind friend, to whom she owed everything, even her miserable life. She trusted still to his honor never to seek to know her real name, nor ever to speak to her of that man if he ever met him. It would do no good to her or to them; it might drive her, for she was not yet quite sure of herself, to do that which she had promised him never to do again.

There was no threat, impatience, or acting in her voice, but he recognized the same dull desperation he had once heard in it, and her eyes, which a moment before were quick and mobile, had become fixed and set. He had no idea of trying to penetrate the foolish secret of her name and relations; he had never had the slightest curiosity, but it struck him now that Stratton might at any time force it upon him. The only way that he could prevent it was to let it be known that, for unexpressed reasons, he would shoot Stratton "on sight." This would naturally restrict any verbal communication between them. Jack's ideas of morality were vague, but his convictions on points of honor were singularly direct and positive.

THREE

Meantime Hamlin and Sophy were passing the outskirts of the town; the open lots and cleared spaces were giving way to grassy stretches, willow copses, and groups of cottonwood and sycamore; and beyond the level of yellowing tules appeared the fringed and raised banks of the river. Half tropical-looking cottages with deep verandas—the homes of early Southern pioneers—took the place of incomplete blocks of modern houses, monotonously alike. In these sylvan surroundings Mr. Hamlin's picturesque rusticity looked less incongruous and more Arcadian; the young girl had lost some of her restraint with her confidences, and lounging together side by side, without the least consciousness of any sentiment in their words or actions, they nevertheless contrived to impress the spectator with the idea that they were a charming pair of pastoral lovers. So strong was this impression that, as they approached Aunt Chloe's laundry, a pretty rose-covered cottage with an enormous white-washed barnlike extension in the rear, the black proprietress herself, standing at the door, called to her husband to come and look at them, and flashed her white teeth in such unqualified commendation and patronage that Mr. Hamlin, withdrawing himself from Sophy's side, instantly charged down upon them.

"If you don't slide the lid back over that grinning box of dominoes of yours and take it inside, I'll just carry Hannibal off with me," he said in a quick whisper, with a half-wicked, half-mischievous glitter in his brown eyes. "That young lady's—*a lady*—do you understand? No riff-raff friend of mine, but a regular *nun*—a saint—do you hear? So you just stand back and let her take a good look round, and rest herself until she wants you." "Two black idiots, Miss Brown," he continued cheerfully in a higher voice of explanation, as Sophy approached, "who think because one of 'em used to shave me and the other saved my life they've got a right to stand at their humble cottage door and frighten horses!"

So great was Mr. Hamlin's ascendancy over his former servants that even this ingenious pleasantry was received with every sign of affection and appreciation of the humorist, and of the profound respect for his companion. Aunt Chloe showed them effusively into her parlor, a small but scrupulously neat and sweet-smelling apartment, inordinately furnished with a huge mahogany center-table and chairs, and the most fragile and meretricious china and glass ornaments on the mantel. But the three jasmine-edged lattice windows opened upon a homely garden of old-fashioned herbs and flowers, and their fragrance filled the room. The cleanest and starchiest of curtains, the most dazzling and whitest of tidies and chair covers, bespoke the adjacent laundry; indeed, the whole cottage seemed to exhale the odors of lavender soap and freshly ironed linen. Yet the cottage was large for the couple and their assistants.

"Dar was two front rooms on de next flo' dat dey never used," explained Aunt Chloe; "friends allowed dat dey could let 'em to white folks, but dey had always been done kep' for Marse Hamlin, ef he ever wanted to be wid his old niggers again."

Jack looked up quickly with a brightened face, made a sign to Hannibal, and the two left the room together.

When he came through the passage a few moments later, there was a sound of laughter in the parlor. He recognized the full, round, lazy, chuckle of Aunt Chloe, but there was a higher girlish ripple that he did not know. He had never heard Sophy laugh before. Nor, when he entered, had he ever seen her so animated. She was helping Chloe set the table, to that lady's intense delight at "Missy's" girlish housewifery. She was picking the berries fresh from the garden, buttering the Sally Lunn, making the tea, and arranging the details of the repast with apparently no trace of her former discontent and unhappiness in either face or manner. He dropped quietly into a chair by the window, and, with the homely scents of the garden mixing with the honest odors of Aunt Chloe's cookery, watched her with an amusement that was as pleasant and grateful as it was strange and unprecedented.

"Now, den," said Aunt Chloe to her husband, as she put the finishing touch to the repast in the plate of doughnuts as exquisitely brown and shining as Jack's eyes were at that moment, "Hannibal, you just come away, and let dem two white quality chillens have dey tea. Dey's done starved, shuah." And with an approving nod to Jack, she bundled her husband from the room.

The door closed; the young girl began to pour out the tea, but Jack remained in his seat by the window. It was a singular sensation which he did not care to disturb. It was no new thing for Mr. Hamlin to find himself at a tête-à-tête repast with the admiring and complaisant fair; there was a cabinet particulier in a certain San Francisco restaurant which had listened to their various vanities and professions of undying faith; he might have recalled certain festal rendezvous with a widow whose piety and impeccable reputation made it a moral duty for her to come to him only in disguise; it was but a few days before that he had been let privately into the palatial mansion of a high official for a midnight supper with a foolish wife. It was not strange, therefore, that he should be alone here, secretly, with a member of that indirect, loving sex. But that he should be sitting there in a cheap Negro laundry with absolutely no sentiment of any kind towards the heavy-haired, freckled-faced country schoolgirl opposite him, from whom he sought and expected nothing, and *enjoying* it without scorn of himself or his companion, to use his own expression, "got him." Presently he rose and sauntered to the table with shining eyes.

"Well, what do you think of Aunt Chloe's shebang?" he asked smilingly.

"Oh, it's so sweet and clean and homelike," said the girl quickly.

At any other time he would have winced at the last adjective. It struck him now as exactly the word.

"Would you like to live here, if you could?"

Her face brightened. She put the teapot down and gazed fixedly at Jack.

"Because you can. Look here. I spoke to Hannibal about it. You can have the two front rooms if you want to. One of 'em is big enough and light enough for a studio to do your work in. You tell that nigger what you want to put in 'em, and he's got my orders to do it. I told him about your painting; said you were the daughter of an old friend, you know. Hold on, Sophy; d—n it all, I've got to do a little gilt-edged lying; but I let you out of the niece business this time. Yes, from this moment I'm no longer your uncle. I renounce the relationship. It's hard," continued the rascal, "after all these years and considering sister Mary's feelings; but, as you seem to wish it, it must be done."

Sophy's steel-blue eyes softened. She slid her long brown hand across the table and grasped Jack's. He returned the pressure quickly and fraternally, even to that half-shamed, half-hurried evasion of emotion peculiar to all brothers. This was also a new sensation; but he liked it.

"You are too, too good, Mr. Hamlin," she said quietly.

"Yes," said Jack cheerfully, "that's what's the matter with me. It isn't natural, and if I keep it up too long it brings on my cough."

Nevertheless, they were happy in a boy and girl fashion, eating heartily, and, I fear, not always decorously; scrambling somewhat for the strawberries, and smacking their lips over the Sally Lunn. Meantime, it was arranged that Mr. Hamlin should inform Miss Mix that Sophy would leave school at the end of the term, only a few days hence, and then transfer herself to lodgings with some old family servants, where she could more easily pursue her studies in her own profession. She need not make her place of abode a secret, neither need she court publicity. She would write to Jack regularly, informing him of her progress, and he would visit her whenever he could. Jack assented gravely to the further proposition that he was to keep a strict account of all the moneys he advanced her, and that she was to repay him out of the proceeds of her first pictures. He had promised also, with a slight mental reservation, not to buy them all himself, but to trust to her success with the public. They were never to talk of what had happened before; she was to begin life anew. Of such were their confidences, spoken often together at the same moment, and with their mouths full. Only one thing troubled Jack: he had not yet told her frankly who he was and what was his reputation. He had hitherto carelessly supposed she would learn it, and in truth had cared little if she did; but it was evident from her conversation that day that by some miracle she was still in ignorance. Unable to tell her himself, he had charged Hannibal to break it to her casually after he was gone.

"You can let me down easy if you like, but you'd better make a square deal of it while you're about it. And," Jack had added cheerfully, "if she thinks after that she'd better drop me entirely, you just say that if she wishes to *stay*, you'll see that I don't ever come here again. And you keep your word about it too, you black nigger, or I'll be the first to thrash you."

Nevertheless, when Hannibal and Aunt Chloe returned to clear away the repast, they were a harmonious party; albeit Mr. Hamlin seemed more content to watch them silently from his chair by the window, a cigar between his lips, and the pleasant distraction of the homely scents and sounds of the garden in his senses. Allusion having been made again to the morning performance of the organ, he was implored by Hannibal to diversify his talent by exercising it on an old guitar which had passed into that retainer's possession with certain clothes of his master's when they separated. Mr. Hamlin accepted it dubiously; it had twanged under his volatile fingers in more pretentious but less innocent halls. But presently he raised his tenor voice and soft brown lashes to the humble ceiling and sang.

"Way down upon the Swanee River,"

discoursed Jack plaintively—

"Far, far away,
Thar's whar my heart is turning ever,
Thar's whar the old folks stay."

The two dusky scions of an emotional race, that had been wont to sweeten its toils and condone its wrongs with music, sat rapt and silent, swaying with Jack's voice until they could burst in upon the chorus. The jasmine vines trilled softly with the afternoon breeze; a slender yellow hammer, perhaps emulous of Jack, swung himself from an outer spray and peered curiously into the room; and a few neighbors, gathering at their doors and windows, remarked that "after all, when it came to real singing, no one could beat those d—d niggers."

The sun was slowly sinking in the rolling gold of the river when Jack and Sophy started leisurely back through the broken shafts of light and across the far-stretching shadows of the cottonwoods. In the midst of a lazy silence they were presently conscious of a distant monotonous throb, the booming of the up boat on the river. The sound came nearer—passed them, the boat itself hidden by the trees; but a trailing cloud of smoke above cast a momentary shadow upon their path. The girl looked up at Jack with a troubled face. Mr. Hamlin smiled reassuringly; but in that instant he had made up his mind that it was his moral duty to kill Mr. Edward Stratton.

FOUR

For the next two months Mr. Hamlin was professionally engaged in San Francisco and Marysville, and the transfer of Sophy from the school to her new home was effected without his supervision. From letters received by him during that interval, it seemed that the young girl had entered energetically upon her new career, and that her artistic efforts were crowned with success. There were a few Indian-ink sketches, studies made at school and expanded in her own "studio," which were eagerly bought as soon as exhibited in the photographer's window—notably by a

florid and inartistic bookkeeper, an old Negro woman, a slangy sta-
bleboy, a gorgeously dressed and painted female, and the bearded second
officer of a river steamboat, without hesitation and without comment.
This, as Mr. Hamlin intelligently pointed out in a letter to Sophy,
showed a general and diversified appreciation on the part of the public.
Indeed, it emboldened her in the retouching of photographs to offer
sittings to the subjects, and to undertake even large crayon copies, which
had resulted in her getting so many orders that she was no longer obliged
to sell her drawings, but restricted herself solely to profitable portraiture.
The studio became known; even its quaint surroundings added to the
popular interest, and the originality and independence of the young
painter helped her to a genuine success. All this she wrote to Jack.
Meantime Hannibal had assured him that he had carried out his instructions by informing "Missy" of his old master's real occupation and
reputation, but that the young lady hadn't "took no notice." Certainly
there was no allusion to it in her letters, nor any indication in her manner.
Mr. Hamlin was greatly, and it seemed to him properly, relieved. And he
looked forward with considerable satisfaction to an early visit to old
Hannibal's laundry.

It must be confessed, also, that another matter, a simple affair of
gallantry, was giving him an equally unusual, unexpected, and absurd
annoyance, which he had never before permitted to such trivialities. In a
recent visit to a fashionable watering place he had attracted the attention
of what appeared to be a respectable, matter-of-fact woman, the wife of a
recently elected rural senator. She was, however, singularly beautiful,
and as singularly cold. It was perhaps this quality, and her evident
annoyance at some unreasoning prepossession which Jack's fascinations
exercised upon her, that heightened that reckless desire for risk and
excitement which really made up the greater part of his gallantry. Nevertheless, as was his habit, he had treated her always with a charming
unconsciousness of his own attentions, and a frankness that seemed
inconsistent with any insidious approach. In fact, Mr. Hamlin seldom
made love to anybody, but permitted it to be made to him with good-
humored deprecation and cheerful skepticism. He had once, quite accidentally, while riding, come upon her when she had strayed from her
own riding party, and had behaved with such unexpected circumspection and propriety, not to mention a certain thoughtful abstraction—it
was the day he had received Sophy's letter—that she was constrained to
make the first advances. This led to a later innocent rendezvous, in
which Mrs. Camperly was impelled to confide to Mr. Hamlin the fact
that her husband had really never understood her. Jack listened with an
understanding and sympathy quickened by long experience of such

confessions. If anything had ever kept him from marriage it was this evident incompatibility of the conjugal relations with a just conception of the feminine soul and its aspirations.

And so eventually this yearning for sympathy dragged Mrs. Camperly's clean skirts and rustic purity after Jack's heels into various places and various situations not so clean, rural, or innocent; made her miserably unhappy in his absence, and still more miserably happy in his presence; impelled her to lie, cheat, and bear false witness; forced her to listen with mingled shame and admiration to narrow criticism of his faults, from natures so palpably inferior to his own that her moral sense was confused and shaken; gave her two distinct lives, but so unreal and feverish that, with a recklessness equal to his own, she was at last ready to merge them both into his. For the first time in his life Mr. Hamlin found himself bored at the beginning of an affair, actually hesitated, and suddenly disappeared from San Francisco.

He turned up a few days later at Aunt Chloe's door, with various packages of presents and quite the air of a returning father of a family, to the intense delight of that lady and to Sophy's proud gratification. For he was lost in a profuse, boyish admiration of her pretty studio, and in wholesome reverence for her art and her astounding progress. They were also amused at his awe and evident alarm at the portraits of two ladies, her latest sitters, that were still on the easels, and in consideration of his half-assumed, half-real bashfulness, they turned their faces to the wall. Then his quick, observant eye detected a photograph of himself on the mantel.

"What's that?" he asked suddenly.

Sophy and Aunt Chloe exchanged meaning glances. Sophy had, as a surprise to Jack, just completed a handsome crayon portrait of himself from an old photograph furnished by Hannibal, and the picture was at that moment in the window of her former patron—the photographer.

"Oh, dat! Miss Sophy jus' put it dar fo' de lady sitters to look at to gib 'em a pleasant 'spresshion," said Aunt Chloe, chuckling.

Mr. Hamlin did not laugh, but quietly slipped the photograph into his pocket. Yet, perhaps it had not been recognized.

Then Sophy proposed to have luncheon in the studio; it was quite "Bohemian" and fashionable, and many artists did it. But to her great surprise Jack gravely objected, preferring the little parlor of Aunt Chloe, the vine-fringed windows, and the heavy respectable furniture. He thought it was profaning the studio, and then—anybody might come in. This unusual circumspection amused them, and was believed to be part of the boyish awe with which Jack regarded the models, the draperies, and the studies on the walls. Certain it was that he was much more at his ease in the parlor, and when he and Sophy were once more alone at their meal, although he ate nothing, he had regained all his old naïveté. Presently he leaned forward and placed his hand fraternally on her arm. Sophy looked up with an equally frank smile.

"You know I promised to let bygones be bygones, eh? Well, I intended it, and more—I intended to make 'em so. I told you I'd never speak to you again of that man who tried to run you off, and I intended that no one else should. Well, as he was the only one who could talk—that meant him. But the cards are out of my hands; the game's been played without me. For he's dead!"

The girl started. Mr. Hamlin's hand passed caressingly twice or thrice along her sleeve with a peculiar gentleness that seemed to magnetize her.

"Dead," he repeated slowly. "Shot in San Diego by another man, but not by me. I had him tracked as far as that, and had my eyes on him, but it wasn't my deal. But there," he added, giving her magnetized arm a gentle and final tap as if to awaken it, "he's dead, and so is the whole story. And now we'll drop it forever."

The girl's downcast eyes were fixed on the table.

"But there's my sister," she murmured.

"Did she know you went with him?" asked Jack.

"No; but she knows I ran away."

"Well, you ran away from home to study how to be an artist, don't you see? Someday she'll find out you *are one*; that settles the whole thing."

They were both quite cheerful again when Aunt Chloe returned to clear the table, especially Jack, who was in the best spirits, with preternaturally bright eyes and a somewhat rare color on his cheeks. Aunt Chloe, who had noticed that his breathing was hurried at times, watched him narrowly, and when later he slipped from the room, followed him into the passage. He was leaning against the wall. In an instant the negress was at his side.

"De Lawdy Gawd, Marse Jack, not *agin?*"

He took his handkerchief, slightly streaked with blood, from his lips and said faintly, "Yes, it came on—on the boat; but I thought the d—d thing was over. Get me out of this, quick, to some hotel, before she knows it. You can tell her I was called away. Say that—" but his breath failed him, and when Aunt Chloe caught him like a child in her strong arms he could make no resistance.

In another hour he was unconscious, with two doctors at his bedside, in the little room that had been occupied by Sophy. It was a sharp attack, but prompt attendance and skillful nursing availed; he rallied the next day, but it would be weeks, the doctors said, before he could be removed in safety. Sophy was transferred to the parlor, but spent most of her time at Jack's bedside with Aunt Chloe, or in the studio with the door open between it and the bedroom. In spite of his enforced idleness and weakness, it was again a singularly pleasant experience to Jack; it amused him to sometimes see Sophy at her work through the open door, and when sitters came—for he had insisted on her continuing her duties as before, keeping his invalid presence in the house a secret—he had all the satisfaction of a mischievous boy in rehearsing to Sophy such of the conversation as could be overheard through the closed door, and speculating on the possible wonder and chagrin of the sitters had they discovered him. Even when he was convalescent and strong enough to be helped into the parlor and garden, he preferred to remain propped up in Sophy's little bedroom. It was evident, however, that this predilection was connected with no suggestion nor reminiscence of Sophy herself. It was true that he had once asked her if it didn't make her "feel like home." The decided negative from Sophy seemed to mildly surprise him. "That's odd," he said; "now all these fixings and things," pointing to the flowers in a vase, the little hanging shelf of books, the knickknacks on the mantel shelf, and the few feminine ornaments that still remained, "look rather like home to me."

So the days slipped by, and although Mr. Hamlin was soon able to walk short distances, leaning on Sophy's arm, in the evening twilight along the river bank, he was still missed from the haunts of dissipated men. A good many people wondered, and others, chiefly of the more irrepressible sex, were singularly concerned. Apparently one of these, one sultry afternoon, stopped before the shadowed window of a photographer's; she was a handsome, well-dressed woman, yet bearing a certain countrylike simplicity that was unlike the restless smartness of the more urban promenaders who passed her. Nevertheless she had halted before Mr. Hamlin's picture, which Sophy had not yet dared to bring home and present to him, and was gazing at it with rapt and breathless attention. Suddenly she shook down her veil and entered the shop. Could the proprietor kindly tell her if that portrait was the work of a local artist?

The proprietor was both proud and pleased to say that *it was!* It was the work of a Miss Brown, a young girl student; in fact, a mere schoolgirl, one might say. He could show her others of her pictures.

Thanks. But could he tell her if this portrait was from life?

No doubt; the young lady had a studio, and he himself had sent her sitters.

And perhaps this was the portrait of one that he had sent her?

No; but she was very popular and becoming quite the fashion. Very probably this gentleman, who, he understood, was quite a public character, had heard of her, and selected her on that account.

The lady's face flushed slightly. The photographer continued. The picture was not for sale; it was only there on exhibition; in fact it was to be returned tomorrow.

To the sitter?

He couldn't say. It was to go back to the studio. Perhaps the sitter would be there.

And this studio? Could she have its address?

The man wrote a few lines on his card. Perhaps the lady would be kind enough to say that he had sent her. The lady, thanking him, partly lifted her veil to show a charming smile, and gracefully withdrew. The photographer was pleased. Miss Brown had evidently got another sitter, and from that momentary glimpse of her face, it would be a picture as beautiful and attractive as the man's. But what was the odd idea that struck him? She certainly reminded him of someone! There was the same heavy hair, only this lady's was golden, and she was older and more mature. And he remained for a moment with knitted brows musing over his counter.

Meantime the fair stranger was making her way towards the river suburb. When she reached Aunt Chloe's cottage, she paused, with the unfamiliar curiosity of a newcomer, over its quaint and incongruous exterior. She hesitated a moment also when Aunt Chloe appeared in the doorway, and, with a puzzled survey of her features, went upstairs to announce a visitor. There was the sound of hurried shutting of doors, of the moving of furniture, quick footsteps across the floor, and then a girlish laugh that startled her. She ascended the stairs breathlessly to Aunt Chloe's summons, found the negress on the landing, and knocked at a door which bore a card marked "Studio." The door opened; she entered; there were two sudden outcries that might have come from one voice.

"Sophonisba!"

"Marianne!"

"Hush."

The woman had seized Sophy by the wrist and dragged her to the window. There was a haggard look of desperation in her face akin to that which Hamlin had once seen in her sister's eyes on the boat, as she said huskily: "I did not know *you* were here. I came to see the woman who had painted Mr. Hamlin's portrait. I did not know it was *you*. Listen! Quick! answer me one question. Tell me—I implore you—for the sake of the mother who bore us both!—tell me—is this the man for whom you left home?"

"No! No! A hundred times no!"

Then there was a silence. Mr. Hamlin from the bedroom heard no more.

An hour later, when the two women opened the studio door, pale but composed, they were met by the anxious and tearful face of Aunt Chloe.

"Lawdy Gawd, Missy—but dey done gone!—bofe of 'em!"

"Who is gone?" demanded Sophy, as the woman beside her trembled and grew paler still.

"Marse Jack and dat fool nigger, Hannibal."

"Mr. Hamlin gone?" repeated Sophy incredulously. "When? Where?"

"Jess now—on de down boat. Sudden business. Didn't like to disturb yo' and yo' friend. Said he'd write."

"But he was ill—almost helpless," gasped Sophy.

"Dat's why he took dat old nigger. Lawdy, Missy, bress yo' heart. Dey both knows aich udder, shuah! It's all right. Dar now, dar dey are; listen."

She held up her hand. A slow pulsation that might have been the dull, labored beating of their own hearts was making itself felt throughout the little cottage. It came nearer—a deep regular inspiration that seemed slowly to fill and possess the whole tranquil summer twilight. It was nearer still—was abreast of the house—passed—grew fainter—and at last died away like a deep-drawn sigh. It was the down boat that was now separating Mr. Hamlin and his protégée, even as it had once brought them together.